P9-EDE-707

HONOR, POWER, RICHES, FAME, AND THE LOVE OF WOMEN

ALSO BY WARD JUST

To What End

A Soldier of the Revolution

Military Men

*The Congressman Who Loved Flaubert
and Other Washington Stories*

Stringer

Nicholson at Large

A Family Trust

HONOR, POWER, RICHES, FAME, AND THE LOVE OF WOMEN

Ward Just

HR

A Henry Robbins Book

E. P. DUTTON · NEW YORK

Grateful acknowledgment is made to the following publishers for permission to reprint the stories in this volume: *Atlantic Monthly, Virginia Quarterly Review, Redbook,* and *New England Magazine.*

For information contact:
E.P. Dutton, 2 Park Avenue, New York, N.Y. 10016

Library of Congress Cataloging in Publication Data

Just, Ward S.
Honor, power, riches, fame, and the love of women.

"A Henry Robbins book."
I. Title.
PZ4.J97Ho [PS3560.U75]   813'.5'4   79–10123

ISBN: 0-525-12675-9

Published simultaneously in Canada by
Clarke, Irwin & Company Limited, Toronto and Vancouver

Designed by Nicola Mazzella

10 9 8 7 6 5 4 3 2 1

First Edition

To my children

Contents

PART I

*Honor, Power, Riches, Fame,
and the Love of Women*

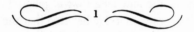

My father, now dead, was mayor of Dement. He served as mayor for three terms, twelve years, then resigned to run for lieutenant governor. None of us wanted him to run, it seemed reckless and eccentric and therefore out of character. We could not understand why he wanted to be lieutenant governor; in Illinois at that time it was an office without visible function. We assumed he wanted to use it as a base or platform for something else, Congress perhaps, or the U.S. Senate, though my father had no love for the federal government or "the East." He was a Taft man and feared socialism.

He was soundly defeated despite a Republican landslide that year, but I know what hurt him most was that he lost Dement. He'd always won his mayoral races by wide margins, and when the returns came in that November Tuesday he was angry and depressed, rejected by his own townspeople. Dement then was much smaller and less turbulent than it is today. I remember its stillness and innocence, a triangle-shaped prairie city isolated from Chicago. It was an unpretentious place of Protestant churches and family farms and small businesses, by its own lights a haven. Its untroubled skin may have concealed a riotous interior, but I doubt it; Dement was unscandalous in all respects. However, it had an inferiority complex common to small towns. Its citizens knew each other too well, and while my father may have been an excellent mayor, that did not qualify him for state office. Better he should stay where he was. I suspect that those who voted against him believed they were doing him a favor, saving him from the heartbreak of the outside world. They were at bottom a suspicious people who perceived Springfield as a glamorous rival and my father's candidacy as a rejection of them. *Aren't we good enough for you?* Dement was fierce to protect its secret self.

It had a reputation as a tough little town, a hard audience. Dement was not hospitable to outsiders, ever. Not long after the war there was a governor who celebrated the land, the cornfields in the fall, finding something hopeful in the mile-long rows of plucked cornstalks, barren and beautiful in Indian summer. He believed that the infinite square of dead fields implied the durability of the land. As the land waited for winter it prepared for spring, leaped ahead one season. It was a definition of confidence and optimism, the fields always fertile and well tended, beautiful and at peace. This governor, campaigning then, made a short speech about it in Dement. He addressed the audience in the gymnasium of the Dement Township High School, standing under the threads of a basketball net.

No one applauded after he spoke; it was as if the words were taken as a prayer or benediction. The crowd dispersed sullenly into the night and the high-minded governor reckoned that he had made an error, given them an unlucky speech that was not understood or appreciated. He had meant to encourage and inspire. This was the heartland after all, and much depended on its stability, its adherence to fixed principles. He wanted them to *persevere.* The governor's friends, sympathetic always, thought that the speech read very well. They told him that the message was necessarily difficult and elusive, and that he was a man ahead of his time. Ideas endured, men did not.

"You can use it as an introduction to your memoirs," one of them said.

But the governor never spoke of it again in the campaign and in Dement people referred to it as that *damn* speech and shook their heads, bewildered and angry. Then they forgot about it and it was never used as an introduction to a book or to anything else. It is remembered only by me; it exists only in my memory, an episode of singular passion.

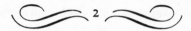

I was my father's driver in his campaign for lieutenant governor and for twenty years I have associated autumn with the special stiff atmosphere of small Illinois towns. Dixon, Alton, Kankakee, Centralia, Mattoon, Waukegan, Bloomington. I see myself still, hunched over the steering wheel of the blue Buick, driving at breakneck speeds down narrow two-lane highways, the highways bisecting fields of corn, soybeans, oats, alfalfa, tame hay. Burma Shave verses on red signs. My father is in the rear seat, revising his speech; his cigar smoke fills the air. Up one rise, down another, up and down, and abruptly a familiar settlement. He says, "Slow down." I remember all of them, the American Legion post in Alton, the Elks Club in Centralia, the old Karcher Hotel in Waukegan. He spoke in a half-shout from notes, his themes as familiar to me as the cigar smoke in the car; standing in the shadows in the rear of the hall, I dozed and counted the house.

In Cook County we always appeared with my father's running mate, the Republican candidate for governor. "In a heavy rain," my father used to say, "you need an umbrella." The candidate for governor, better known and better financed and organized, was my father's umbrella in the hostile and unfamiliar suburbs of Chicago. He was a willing umbrella until mid-October, when it became clear that he was running well and would win and my father was running poorly and would lose. Then we were on our own and the final weeks of the campaign were desperate and unbearably lonely. The campaign manager returned to his law practice in De Kalb, and the two advance men drifted off to other, more promising campaigns. Even my mother seemed to lose her enthusiasm and my father's telephone calls home became less frequent. The campaign became an erratic odyssey with no inner logic, like a love affair doomed and out of control. In the car, my father and I barely spoke; as he sensed defeat he withdrew, growing colder and angrier and more passionate with each new bit of depressing evidence.

Yet he did not break stride, he threw his full energies into his manic courtship, rising at dawn and never retiring before midnight. Reaching out to audiences, he could not stop talking. He spoke of the enormous odds he faced; he said his advisers were discouraging. But odds could be beaten and advisers were often wrong. In any case, he would not quit; he was not a quitter, they had to understand that. But his cadences, insistent and irregular, irritated his listeners; he seemed to be daring them to reject him. He constructed his speeches, sentence by heavy sentence, during the long drives between towns. He'd mutter bits and pieces of the harangue and then, under his breath—"shit," or "you whore," pronounced *hoor*. The last week we worked the Republican counties downstate, speaking before any crowd that would listen. Applause, any applause, no matter how perfunctory, would buoy his spirits. We would return to the car and he would speak briefly with animation —*Good crowd, I got to them that time, we'll make hay here. . . .* Then he would wind down, physically sink into the Buick's cushions, and presently I would hear his pen scratching across the yellow pad. Fresh proposals for the next speech.

And me? All of it was newly minted. I was twenty, just graduated from college, fascinated by the process. I absorbed it like a sponge, becoming a connoisseur of effects. I listened, and when I could not listen

I watched, and when I could not watch I closed my eyes and imagined it, hearing and seeing in my mind only. I observed his maneuvers in small Illinois towns, a gruff word to the men, a shy smile to the ladies, then an earnest lecture from the podium. Acknowledging the cheers at the beginning of each speech, he would clasp his hands above his head like a prizefighter. I watched the others watching him and I knew instantly the moment he lost them. I noticed the moment they grew restless and I was vexed that he did not know it. I knew it, it was perfectly obvious, why didn't he? I watched the smiles of the audience dissolve, their mouths grow tight with disapproval. Too serious. I believe my old man was too serious because in every other way his views were theirs. It wasn't politics that divided him and the audience, it was passion. He wanted it so much.

The Sunday afternoon before the election he spoke at an I.O.O.F. picnic in Bloomington. We were to spend the night, then drive to Dement the next day for the final appearance of the campaign. En route that morning I decided to break silence and tell him what I thought. I tried to tell him why I thought he wasn't connecting. I suggested that he tread a little lighter. Open with a joke, I said. In the Midwest, people came to political rallies to be entertained. Entertain them a little. . . .

He listened in silence. Then he said, "You drive. It'll be over in a day and then you can go home to your friends. I appreciate your driving. It must be very *boring* for you, these little towns that you don't like. What did you call them the other day? Tank towns. There's only one more day, and then you'll be home. You can do what you want, then." I could hear him breathing hard, believing that he had put me down in a decisive way. Except we both knew that he spoke the truth. I was bored, I hated the small towns. And I did want to go home, if only to prepare to leave for somewhere else.

Autumn was almost over, the trees were bare and the fields stripped, desiccated in a hot spell. It was warm in Bloomington. Children skylarked on bikes and a softball game was in progress in the worn diamond.

It might have been mid-August except for the look of the trees and the haze in the sky, and the smell of burning leaves. I remember standing at the rear of the picnic grounds, leaning against a tree, listening to my father. He was attacking Communists in government and drawing applause for it. The applause seemed to encourage him, because he continued on that theme for thirty minutes, describing himself as the Number One Target of the Communists. Of course, by then he'd lost the audience.

A girl in a print dress came over to me, carrying two bottles of Hamm's beer. She offered me one and I took it and thanked her and we stood there a moment, saying nothing. I could not place her; she had been one of a blur of introductions when we'd arrived. She asked me if I was having a good time in Bloomington and I nodded politely. Then she smiled and gestured toward the stage and my father, talking.

"That's your dad, isn't it?"

I nodded; it was suddenly embarrassing and tiresome to me. I was tired, sick of the campaign; sick of the small towns and afternoon picnics; sick of small talk; sick of being a chauffeur; sick of watching my father try and fail. He had completely lost the audience now and was talking into a din of conversation. The truth was, I believed I had no more to learn from this campaign.

"Well, that's *my* dad," she said. "The other one."

"The president?"

"None other," she said. "The president of the I.O.O.F.—the eee-oof." He was seated to the left of my father on the stage. He seemed to be the only one who was truly listening. She was smiling broadly now and leaning toward me, as if sharing a secret. "He is in his second term as president of the . . . Odd Fellows." She drained her beer and we listened to my father; his speech was winding down and his voice was blurred. She said, "My father hates Communists. Always has."

"Always?"

"Since he was an itty-bitty baby," she said.

"Well." I could think of nothing else to say.

"He thinks they are running Springfield. Governor Stevenson brought them in and hid them in the various departments. They are like time bombs, set to explode at intervals. They are there now, and when the Kremlin gives the signal they'll take it over. My father has specific evidence relating to the infiltration of the Department of Motor Vehicles. He believes the Reds are interfering with auto registrations." She spoke as if reading from a prepared text. "He believes that unless your father is elected lieutenant governor, Springfield will be the first to go." She nodded gravely and moved off to a table nearby. This was apparently a table of friends, for she fetched two more bottles of beer from the ice chest and returned. My father had warned me not to speak to strangers. He believed the Democrats would do anything to compromise him, and he also feared the press, specifically reporters from the Chicago *Sun-Times* and the St. Louis *Post-Dispatch*. He'd said to me, "They'd like nothing better than to print some stupid remark you might make, so mind your p's and q's and don't say anything to anyone you aren't sure of. Check with me first."

She said, "How about yours?"

"He believes they are in the schools," I said.

"Underground?"

"Yes," I said. "They are underground men."

"Any particular department?"

"History mainly," I lied. "He has made a study of the . . . texts." I was improvising now, having fun. "He believes that the first step is a falsification of history. He believes they are altering the documents." I looked at her. "He intends to put a stop to it, after he is elected."

She nodded uh huh.

"I do not know what steps two and three are."

"Well," she said. "It's obvious they would be concealed."

"No doubt," I said.

She said, "The Communists. Is that why he is running for lieutenant governor?"

I looked at her and shrugged, it was all hopeless. And it was no longer funny. This day in November, unseasonably warm; I was in shirt sleeves and perspiring but she looked cool and fresh. I surveyed the picnic grounds, the tables laden with food and drink; the two men on the platform, the one talking, the other listening. No one else was listening, my father was talking to an audience of one. The softball game continued, hits, errors, base runners sliding in clouds of dust. Dust rose over the diamond. Behind the third-base line was a mound of leaves, a mound five feet high; I wanted to go roll in it. Nearby there was laughter and I could hear a phrase or two of my father's. *An uphill fight,* he was saying. Then: *We must be vigilant.* I could not imagine what I was doing there on a picnic grounds in Bloomington, Illinois, and told her that.

"We are here because they are," she said, gesturing toward the platform. "Isn't that clear enough?"

"No," I said.

"That's because you haven't thought about it."

"I was kidding about the history," I said. "It's just a vague thing with him, the Communists. He's a good guy, really. He'd be all right as lieutenant governor." I paused. Why was I saying this? "The Communists are just a momentary thing. He's worked like hell, he's tired." She was looking at me with wide blue eyes. "He wants it so damn badly." Then, "He knew it would be a popular thing with this crowd, so he's talking about the Communists. It could as easily be about farm price supports or . . . anything else." I shrugged. "Himself. The odds against." I suddenly felt very sorry for my father, and angry at myself.

She touched my arm and smiled sadly. "I wish I could say the same," she said in a low voice. "He really believes it. Poor old bastard."

Suddenly we were on a different plane altogether. I was surprised at the word, it was not a word girls used then about their fathers. But she said it with affection; there was no rancor in her voice. I knew we were in agreement and I was happy she was there. I was happy we were together, drinking beer and talking.

"Hell," I said. "If it isn't communism it's something else. It doesn't matter anyhow."

"It matters," she said. "That's the sad part." Then: "You looked so sad when I walked over here—"

"This has not been my best day. Or his, either."

"You are not enjoying yourself?"

"No."

"And you haven't told me why he is running."

I could feel the first effects of the beer, and of her. But I remembered the warning. Anything could happen in this campaign. Enemies were everywhere. "You're not a reporter, are you?" She looked at me hard, hurt, not knowing whether I was serious or not. I quickly added, "A Democrat? A conscious dedicated agent of the conspiracy?" She smiled and moved her head, her hair brushing my shoulder. All my defenses went at once and I wanted very badly to tell this girl about the past two months, all of it, every rally and chicken dinner and Main Street walkaround. And my own careful observations, effects crowding my memory.

I said, "Whoever you are, I don't know why he is running for office. None of us knows, and I'm not certain that he knows; all he knows for sure is that he *wants* it. But it doesn't make any difference because he's going to lose. Then he will go back to his insurance agency in Dement and I will go with him, until the first of the year. Lewis and Sons Insurance. Fire, theft, casualty. We have known he would lose for three weeks, but we never speak of it; he speaks of odds against, and of prevailing in the face of pessimism. It gives him confidence, God knows why. We both know he will lose but we don't say it. We have traveled from one end of this lousy state to the other, driving two, three hundred miles a day. I drive and daydream; he sits in the back seat, revising his speeches. We try to make at least two speeches a day, but lately it has been three speeches. Never the same speech, understand that: fresh crowd, fresh speech. Since the campaign manager left and the advance men joined other campaigns it's been very difficult. He has to make the arrangements himself, he has to plead with people like your father. He is popular with the Legion and with the I.O.O.F., so he can usually get a hearing. I have seen a hundred Legion posts in this state and I can recite the Pledge of Allegiance backwards in my sleep. I have met every Legion official in the state of Illinois and I want nothing more now than for a new war to break out. Except that this would be a war by invitation only to men over the age of forty. Restricted to members of the American Legion. Every morning before the assault they could recite the Pledge of Allegiance among themselves, tell some war stories to get in the mood, and then pick up their bayonets and charge the . . . Department of Motor Vehicles. This place, whoever you are, is *insane*. The legionnaires, they're a genuine National Guard, they're making Illinois safe for—"

"History," she said.

"Yes, exactly that. So that is what I have been doing for more than two months, and tomorrow, when this is over, I will return to the office. I will write casualty insurance. Then, at Christmastime, I will take my savings and leave, God knows where. . . ." I paused; her friends at the table were looking at me strangely. She caught my hand and held it, squeezing. She was grinning, her eyes bright.

"Sandra," she said.

"Tom Lewis," I said.

"Come on."

"Where?"

She was still holding my hand. "Home," she said. "Geez, you really got wound up. That was terrific."

"I can't—"

"He can find his way to the hotel. My father will look after him, they'll have a lot to talk about. It's all right, you don't have to worry."

As we walked away from the picnic grounds I could hear scattered applause. She moved close against me, waving casually to the group at the table. Then she began to run. We both ran away from the picnic grounds, our feet slapping the cement sidewalks. Bloomington reminded me of Dement, identical frame houses, porches facing similar streets, blinds drawn within. It was very quiet in the streets. Each house was shaded by a tree, an elm or a hickory. It was as if a single architect had designed both towns; perhaps he was a circuit-riding architect like a judge or a physician. I knew without being told which houses belonged to professional people and which belonged to merchants or shopkeepers.

Dusk was coming on and we ran faster and faster beneath the bare branches of the huge trees, cutting across lawns and through alleys, still holding hands. Leaves were piled on front lawns and in the gutters and the scent of burning was in the air. We ran for three blocks and then we walked, out of breath and laughing. Her face was damp and we were both perspiring; my shirt was stuck to my back. I still carried my bottle of Hamm's and handed it to her. She took a long swallow, draining it, and tossed the bottle into the gutter where it fell soundlessly among the leaves. My thumb was wet from the lip of the bottle. We walked for a while, talking, and then we ran on. She tripped once and fell, skinning her knee; there was a little blood and dirt where she had fallen and tears jumped to her eyes. She daubed at it with a handkerchief and said it was nothing, it would leave no mark, and didn't hurt much. We began to run again. The town passed by me in a blur, the streets undulating. Now the houses were close together and bushes obscured their facades; brittle ivy, pale green and flecked with brown, hung in dry patches from the brick and the clapboard. Vacant lots were thick with vegetation, overgrown with high weeds and scrub oak. Tree branches touched over the narrow deserted streets, natural trellises spanning the concrete. From somewhere nearby I heard faint laughter and familiar voices. I could not identify them and I touched her arm and we both halted, skidding to a stop, listening; it was the radio, metallic voices drifting through open windows in the evening stillness. I looked at my watch, it was Jack Benny, had to be; Benny and Rochester and a studio audience. The voices were more distinct now as other radios were switched on; I sensed movement behind the windows. I heard two words, *Mistah Benny. . . .* Darkness was gathering quickly now, it seemed to me that we had run for hours down these streets; the trees were black against the lawns and there were few lights inside the houses. In the heart of Bloomington, in darkest Illinois, there was only the radio. I laughed, gazing skyward; what were the first words heard in this heart of darkness? *Mistah Benny* . . .

She tugged at my arm, impatient to be off. We picked up the pace and were running again, the picnic grounds far behind now. We drifted easily down the sidewalks and across lawns. Then we were moving up the stairs of a front porch, taking the steps two at a time. The screen door banged and we were inside. The house was cool and ablaze with light. Every light in the house was on. We stood in the middle of the parlor, panting; I bent at the waist, trying to catch my breath. The light hurt our eyes, and she methodically moved around the parlor switching off the lamps. Presently we were in darkness again. She laughed for no reason and left me a moment, disappearing through the swinging door into the kitchen. I heard the icebox open and close and the water run and her humming, and then she was back.

"No beer," she said. She took my hand and we mounted the stairs. They were narrow and uncarpeted and we bumped the walls as we climbed. I put the palm of my hand on the small of her back and felt her heat. She laughed softly. Her room was at the top of the stairs, the door closed. We burst through it and I led her straight to her bed. We fell on it together and embraced for a long moment. It was very still, the only sound was the rustle of our clothing; we did not kiss right away, it was enough lying together on the bed, our bodies touching everywhere. Then we kissed, delicately, lips barely touching. I kissed her chin and her eyes and then we lay apart for a moment. Her eyes were closed, her long lashes touching her cheeks, her mouth upturned at the edges and slightly parted. I felt her breathing, her breasts rising; I timed my own breathing to be in tune with her. I wanted no part of us in disharmony. She ran her hand slowly down my cheek, caressing very lightly; I did the same. Her hair, light brown and thick and soft as down, was in curly disarray. I smoothed it and took two strands and arranged them around her ears. Her eyes popped open then and I found myself in her pupils; her eyes were like mirrors, my face convex, my grave expression distorted. I moved closer to her and we kissed again, this time longer and deeper. She smelled wonderfully. Her hands went around my back and squeezed and kept squeezing. I drew her as close to me as I was able, wildly happy at that moment. She was not slight but she felt slight, small-boned and slender, my arms around her, our legs twined like vines. We lay together in the big soft bed, arms around each other. Time suspended itself. I could not stop touching her.

After a while she pushed me away and we lay six inches apart and talked. I talked about everything in my life, it seemed to me there was nothing I might say that she would not understand. We made jokes about the conspiracy: Was it true that Tom Dewey took his orders from Moscow? We joked and then we talked seriously, and then we kissed some more. I would tell her everything that mattered to me, every fact and emotion, then I would listen as she explained her life to me. We were hearing our own harmonies, mounting the scale as if it were a staircase, each story improving the one before. We prepared the ground for disclosures, things we had never discussed with anyone. I told her repeatedly that I could not believe this was happening, I did not believe in chance encounters. Was it true that she was an undercover agent for the *Post-Dispatch,* anxious to pry compromising information from the son of the candidate?

I listened to her breathing. We saw each other dimly in the blackness of the room; occasionally I would squeeze my eyelids shut to see her in my mind only; then I would open up and find there was no difference. I imagined her to perfection, every detail. She described her life: her mother was dead, there were just she and her father. Ever since the death of her mother she felt . . . at loose ends. Literally, she did not feel whole; she felt her emotions were leaking away through her nerve ends. One day she would awaken and find herself parched, dry as dust. What was there for her in Bloomington? She would succeed at something, make no mistake; she did not intend to stay in this house. But she felt her life was muffled, smothered in cotton batting; all escape routes were blocked, she was wrapped in mufflers. She could not escape from the place or reconcile herself to it, either one. Bloomington: it was supposed to be the center of the continent, one could gaze east or west with equal ease; but she did not find it so. She said that the walls of Bloomington were higher and thicker than the walls of any prison. The truth was, she was afraid to leave. She said she noticed me right away at the picnic and knew from the look on my face that I felt as she did; she had an instinct for looks, it was an instinct she'd always had. I was living under the same conditions, wasn't I? In that way we were brothers, except being a man it would be easier for me; it would always be easier. And I had some money and she did not. Up close, her mouth almost touching mine, she whispered that we were both on bivouac. She chuckled dryly; we were on night watch surrounded by enemies. We laughed together, improving on that image. We discussed the weapons we'd need and the tactics we'd use to exfiltrate the prairie. Passion, she said finally; that was all there was. It was evidence of life. She looked at me fiercely in the dark, her fingers on my chest. Not sex, she said; passion. There was a difference. Then she smiled and added, Though not always.

I took her hand and kissed it; I was bound to her. It seemed to me that she knew everything, her understanding was limitless. I told her she'd cast a spell. We were so close in spirit now that there was no difference between us at all. She rolled over on top of me, burying her face in my neck; she was murmuring something, I did not hear what it was. Light as feathers she slipped out of her dress, her skin shining in the faint light from the street. Her hair fell to her shoulders in loops and her eyes were open and glittering. I moved slowly, as slowly as time itself. *One,* she said. And again, *One.*

I heard a noise in the street and presently the front door slammed and we both sat upright. We could hear conversation and then, quickly, the clink of ice cubes in glasses. I looked at her: What do we do now? She smiled ruefully, hugging herself, her arms covering her breasts. Then she put her arms down and just sat for a moment, looking at me with a smile. She whispered, *It's a farce. Everything collapses into farce.* She sighed and climbed over me and stepped on tiptoe to the door and listened, one leg bent, her arms at her sides. I watched her from the bed, every movement. Then she motioned me over and we sat on the floor together and listened.

It was her father and mine, both mid-drunk, sitting in the parlor, their voices just louder than they needed to be. It was evident that they thought the house was empty. She lay in my arms on the floor and we listened to them.

Her father was telling mine that he was a great American. There weren't many left, Truman had ruined it. The Communists were everywhere now, they were like termites eating away at the foundations of the house. The house could collapse at any time and Eisenhower was too dumb to do anything about it. "Never trust a general," he said. But thank God the polls had Eisenhower winning and with any luck in two days they'd be rid of the haberdasher forever. He and Hiss and Harry Dexter White and the whole rotten barrel. General Vaughan, the five-percenters. Bad as Eisenhower was, at least he wasn't Stevenson. They all knew about Stevenson, he had grown up in Bloomington and owned a piece of the local rag, the newspaper. As governor he had reduced Illinois, Land of Lincoln, to a Poland or a Czechoslovakia. Illinois was no different from any of the satellite Russian states. When Stevenson used the state police to break up the gambling he had served notice and signaled his intent: it was to establish a KGB in Springfield, a secret police. J. Edgar Hoover knew all about it but was powerless to act. Stevenson had tried to dismantle the National Guard but was prevented by the many scandals. The cigarette stamp tax scandal, the horsemeat scandal, and the others. There were too many scandals to count. Haha, he said. I heard a good one the other day. Man goes into a meat market to buy hamburger and the butcher asks him if he wants it win, place, or show.

I heard my father grunt and sigh, and then a fresh tinkle of ice cubes. The voice droned on. I knew my father had disconnected from the conversation and was thinking private thoughts.

Her father said, You know he's a fairy.

My father said nothing. I tried to picture him in the chair, stiff and morose and exhausted and pulling on a highball; and listening to the president of the I.O.O.F. beat up Adlai Stevenson. My father had always described the governor as a bad politician, often feckless and weird in his choice of friends and associates; but not a bad man.

That is what they say, her father said. And not only that (his voice lowered to a confidential level), but he has a woman in the mansion. There's a woman who's in residence around the clock to service him.

Her face was buried in my chest, her shoulders were shaking with laughter. Her hands beat a little tattoo on my back. She whispered to me that much of this material was new to her. Her father had hinted at private scandal but had never spelled it out. Too *risqué.* She giggled.

Well, her father said at last, here's to victory on Tuesday.

I heard the clink of glasses and my father clear his throat. I was waiting for him to argue, though I guessed he would not. He hated references to private lives, and I never heard him gossip. He was a practical man and hated confrontation. He would know there was no convincing argument he could make. I was amused at the lunacy of it, Stevenson a secret voluptuary, saturnalias in the mansion at Springfield.

My father said, "I'm still wondering where my son is."

"He and my daughter went off together. They were talking during the speech. They're all right, don't worry about them. She's probably showing him around the town, there's quite a good deal of local history here in Bloomington. She'll take good care of him, you shouldn't worry."

"I'm not worried," my father said. There was a strange timbre to his voice, a rattle that I had never heard before. "But we've got to leave early; there's a rally in Dement at noon and I've got a speech at night. The Elks."

"Fine people."

"Yes, I've been an Elk for—twenty years."

"Give it to them hard, Giles. Tell them about the screwballs in Springfield. I can tell you, when you get there, you have only to call on me if you need any help in Bloomington. I can give you support. I can do *things*. I'll do anything I can for you, anything at all to help clean up the mess—" Her father abruptly stopped talking. There was an awkward silence, punctuated by sounds I could not identify. I leaned forward, my ear against the door jamb. I heard *unh unh unh,* as if a pillow were being punched. There were no other sounds, just those. It was my father, and I understood in a frozen second that he was crying. I could not move, I was paralyzed; my hands fell away from her.

"Well," her father began. It was an awful moment.

"Shit," my father said. He blew his nose. A thick silence seemed to spread through the house, the air suddenly compressed and made heavy. I imagined the other man turning away in embarrassment. "There isn't much for a lieutenant governor to do," my father said slowly. He was not prepared to acknowledge that he had been weeping. He spoke in a broken undertone, to himself alone. "There isn't much to the job, it's a largely ceremonial thing. Ribbon-cuttings. Banquets." Then, in his familiar voice: "Guess we'd better get back to the hotel, get some sleep. Heavy day tomorrow."

"I guess we better," the other said stiffly. I could have killed him, his tone was so condescending.

"I want to be there by noon, not a minute later." The other one was silent. "Goddammit, if you'd pay attention, stop dreaming, keep your eyes on the road. The other day, outside Alton, that semi—" I realized then that he was talking to me. He believed I was in the room with him. "You've got to concentrate. Good driving is just concentration, no more and no less. Understand where you are, where you're going. Know the rules of the road and obey them." Her father coughed and I could hear him rise. "Christ, to have to depend on *you.*" Then he was silent, and I could feel—*feel*—the atmosphere change.

He said, "I believe now that I should have stayed in the agency.

My three boys are there. It's a good agency, none better in Dement. The other two understand about business. The one with me here now, it was important for him to see the state. His mother felt it would be helpful to him to see all the state. Her people came from around Centralia. He's been my driver on the . . . campaign. It's a responsible post, because everywhere I go I've got to be on time. Punctual. But he's restless. He's very much like his uncle, my brother. Two peas in a pod, they should both be in Chicago. They're *sophisticated.*" He spat the word out, an obscenity to him.

"I can take you back to the hotel."

"You know," my father said. "Stevenson isn't the worst of the lot by any means." He spoke very softly, it was difficult for me to hear. It was just a statement, I could tell that he would not pursue it.

"Well, I suppose he's not as bad as Williams. Compared to Williams, he's all right." The other was making a concession; I relaxed. I had had a feeling there would be a fight between them, and I would have to go down and break it up.

"Williams is in the pocket of Reuther," my father said. "Reuther owns him. That Reuther's a cold one."

"A menace to America. Soapy Williams is a screwball, always was, always will be." Her father went on to describe social and political subversion in the state of Michigan.

But we were no longer listening. Or I wasn't. I'd had no idea it went so deep: my father in tears; his evident contempt for me. I wanted the sounds to go away, but they would not. I had eavesdropped and I had heard him. I had *heard.* It was as if I'd stolen something from him and now it belonged to me forever. She lay quietly, watching me, her eyes bright and mournful. My confusion was complete. I vaguely remember the screen door slamming and, later, her father returning to the house. We sat in silence for many minutes, my father's words repeating themselves in my brain; I was numb, unable to sort out my feelings. I did not know what to think. She said, "Something like that happened to my father about a year ago. I was in the kitchen, I heard him upstairs—" I shook my head sharply, I didn't want to hear it.

I'd heard too much already. I didn't want to listen to anything of a private nature between her and her father. It was midnight when we crept out of her room and down the stairs. Her father was asleep in the big wing-back chair, a half-empty highball on the table beside him. All the downstairs lights were blazing. He was snoring gently, his face slack. Whiskey fumes filled the room. I smiled, though there was nothing comical about it. She moved quickly to his side and took the glass of stale whiskey and put it on another table. The resemblance between them was striking; I had not noticed it before. In repose his face was almost feminine, and the look around his eyes was identical to his daughter's.

We quietly left the house and stood on the front lawn, out of the light. A breeze had come up and it was chilly and very dark. We pressed against each other, I could feel goose bumps on her arms. I could see the streetlights at the corner but nothing beyond. She looked at me and smiled apologetically, her eyes lowered. She said, "Really, he's helpless. Helpless since his wife died. It was odd because they did not seem to've needed each other in life." I was not listening to her. She said she wanted to drive me to the hotel but she didn't drive. She'd never learned, no one had taught her. She was twenty years old and a nondriver, and that was unheard of. It's a long way, she said; maybe twenty blocks. I told her the truth: I didn't mind.

We walked off to the corner and it was like entering a tunnel. I was entirely absorbed by what I'd heard, my father's words mingling with the image of Sandra's body; her beauty was breathtaking. I thought, What was there about this country? This hard place in the heart of the nation. The carapace of control was so thin. It looked hard as iron but the looks were deceptive. Everything beneath was confused and in turmoil, dry on the outside and wet underneath. My father *in tears.* I could hardly believe it. His disappointment, the ragged edge of his emotions; I had always thought of him as a stoic. There was just his voice, gone to pieces, and the thickening atmosphere. I had always thought of him pursuing a line of duty.

"This place," she said. "It's surprising sometimes."

Something, perhaps it was the dark street and the prospect of a twenty-block walk, had made me cautious. I wanted very much to be alone and I did not want or need the help or sympathy of anyone. I said, "Yes."

She said, "It's all right."

I said, "No, it isn't." I was angry at her father.

"He's tired, he's been campaigning for—what? Two months, three months? They get worn out—"

"Three months," I said. I wanted to remain with the obvious explanations.

"Well, there you are."

"It surprised me," I said slowly. "I thought he had reconciled himself. . . . I knew it meant a lot. I knew that. But I thought he was stronger. . . ."

She paused a moment, looking at me. "Why should he be? You're not, I'm not." Her voice was very clear in the darkness. "Why isn't he entitled—"

"Defeated," I said. I was talking to myself now, still with the obvious things. "He sounded defeated."

"That's cruel," she said sharply. "That's the cruelest thing I've ever heard. Don't you understand anything about these men?"

"No, I'm not cruel," I said. I was honestly bewildered, I thought I had merely stated the truth.

"You don't understand anything about them." She put her hands on my shoulders. "They're trying to break out, same as we are. They know it isn't working, none of it. With my father, it's the Reds. With yours, it's you. Same difference. No difference."

"I don't have anything to do with this," I said thickly.

She sighed, exasperated. "Yes," she said. "You do."

"No," I said. "Definitely not." I took her hand. I wanted nothing more than to be away from there. It was so dark I could barely see her face, or the outlines of her body. But I was able to see her expression in my mind's eye, her clear sad eyes and the downward sweep of her eyebrows. I wanted to be away from that street and the house, and the man asleep in the wing-back chair.

She smiled and kissed me lightly. She said, "The Reds. You. Subversives. Problems to be solved. Think of it that way, will you?"

I told her I would write.

She smiled, then laughed. "Be good," she said.

We were at the corner. I was to follow her street straight into town. The hotel was in the center of town. The street sloped and I could see little puddles of light for perhaps six blocks, then the street curved down and away. Light filtered through the bare branches of the trees. It was black as hell, the blackest night I've ever seen. We kissed in the dark, leaning against the rough bark of a hickory tree and feeling the chill. Her body was wonderfully soft and supple. Then we broke and she turned away without a word and walked back up the street to her house, her arms hugging her body to ward off the cold. Indian summer was over.

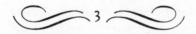

I did not leave Dement for another year, and when I did I went to Washington. Sandra and I saw each other twice afterward and we corresponded for a while and then gave it up. The episode in Bloomington remains an isolated event. Sometimes when I think about it I am not sure that it happened at all. (But I know it did.) Three years later I was married and when I explained it to my wife she said that everyone had a similar episode in the past, and ambiguous memories about it. She said that collapse was inevitable because the relationship was too intense; each is heavily dependent on the other and the dependencies do not fit. They almost never do. Too taut, exactly like a rubber band; it's pulled too far and it snaps. Expectations are too high. I said that it had been an enchanting experience, at least one half of it had; I said I would not trade that half for anything. She smiled sympathetically. Just see that it doesn't happen again, she said. Then, seriously: Passion wears out, you know. It doesn't endure. It can't be maintained, it exists only as a peak among valleys. We shall see, I said lightly. An odd fact: I never thought to inquire about *her* "similar experience," who he was and what she made of it, and she never thought to volunteer.

My brothers live in Dement still, managing the agency. This is a characteristic of the Midwest, small businesses handed down from father to son. It is particularly true of insurance, the law, and medicine. Of course, it is a reach for immortality, the agency or law firm or practice outliving and overwhelming the family serving it. The business acquires a weight and personality and growth of its own, often more formidable than the family. No wonder that the office is casually referred to as "the plant." In Dement the mortality rate was about fifty-fifty into the second generation. Attorneys are consulted to keep the businesses alive, control exquisitely balanced among families and generations. Usually the sons do not have the singleness of purpose of the fathers, or the stamina. The times intervene. The attorneys speak of these businesses reverently, as necessary keystones of the civic edifice. Dement, one of them explained to me once, was very much an insider's town. "Those of us here who run things, we don't have to finish sentences. . . ." He wanted to see that Dement remained an insider's town.

Lewis and Sons Insurance was one of the rare ones. My two brothers worked hard and expanded the business, and today it is three times as large as it was when my father died. My brothers and I do not communicate often because there is considerable bitterness between us. Our father bequeathed the agency in thirds, which means that I share in the profits though I do no work for the agency. I have had to hire an attorney in Dement to see that my interest is protected, and that the profits are distributed equally. My brothers have managed to increase the business each year but the profits do not grow; they are stable because the salaries and expense accounts rise. Last year, my share of the swag was ten thousand dollars. Meanwhile, Brother Warren bought a condominium in Fort Lauderdale and Brother Bill a thirty-five-foot Chris-Craft. Each of them takes seventy thousand dollars a year out of the business. They say (through their attorney), We're doing the work, we'll reap the profits. I say (through mine), Fine, as long as I get the ten thousand per annum, no less. This is a situation common in family businesses. Dividends, as everyone knows, are fully taxable to the corporation and to the individuals receiving them. It is the most expensive way to extract money from a business, and therefore it is not often done. The preferred method is to establish "consultancies" or bogus titles through which a family member can receive a salary. However, that is not desirable for me. Regularly, once a year, I get a letter from my brothers' mouthpiece urging me to "do something about this." Excessive taxation of corporate profits threatens the health of our capitalistic system, the attorney says. "We would hope you would use your position in a constructive way."

They have tried on numerous occasions to buy me out but I refuse to sell. For reasons I do not entirely understand, I want to keep a foot in Dement. The family has been there for four generations and I have not been anxious to cut the last cord. The only way I know to keep a foot in is to retain the stock, come what may. (Also, they have not offered me a fair price.) I return once a year for the formalities of the board of directors' meeting. There are five of us in attendance, I and my two brothers, the corporation counsel, and my uncle, who is eighty-two and in failing health. It is a stiff, formal ceremony that never consumes more than thirty minutes. President Warren Lewis confines himself to a recitation of numbers: new accounts and dollar volume at the bottom line. Details are scarce. All motions are proposed by the attorney and seconded by Treasurer Bill Lewis and passed unanimously by those of us at the table. They have the votes and they know it; I know it too and am resentful. We meet in the conference room at the agency; suspended on wires over the door is a ghastly portrait of the founder, my father, his light eyes wide and staring as if at a vision or apparition.

His last years were spent playing golf and the artist drew him in a white shirt against a bilious horizon, a suggestion of fairways. President Warren sounds remarkably like the old man, and in his middle age has even come to resemble him (he is big). Afterward I have lunch with my brothers and their wives and the attorney and his wife and my aged uncle, and then I am driven to the Dement airport to take the commuter flight to O'Hare and then a jet to Washington.

For some years I have been a congressman from a district in upstate New York.

Somewhere (in fact it is Lecture Twenty-three of the General Introduction) Freud describes the artist as one who desires "honor, power, riches, fame, and the love of women" but lacks the ways and means of attaining them. Frustrated, he attempts to satisfy himself by making fantasies which, according to Freud, represent repressed infantile longings. The great analyst then goes on to describe the artist's "puzzling ability" to reproduce his fantasies so persuasively that other disappointed souls are—consoled. I believe that the aim of art is consolation, and it is the aim of politics as well; the artist and the politician are brothers, and their situations essentially ironic. Freud: the artist "wins gratitude and admiration for himself and so, by means of his imagination, achieves the very things which had at first only an imaginary existence for him: honor, power, and the love of women." Similarly, the politician, his "program" and his "image." Thus we win *through* fantasy that which before we could win only *in* fantasy. The way back from imagination to reality is art. I found Lecture Twenty-three in my last year at the university and have never forgotten it. Inspired by Freud's promise, I planned for myself a career as an artist. But I did not have the temperament for it, and it soon became clear to me that my life would be public. I wanted to touch people, and be touched in return; that was how I explained it. I wanted things out front where I could see them and I had no taste at all for reliving, if only through memory, my rather ordinary childhood. Tom Lewis the child lives still in Dement. Tom Lewis the man is a Washingtonian.

Politics is a delusive trade. In his secret heart a successful politician believes he is truly loved. Not merely supported or well liked but loved. He is father to a constituency of children, and while some of the children may be obstinate or disobedient, none of them is beyond salvation. When a politician loses an election he cannot believe it is because he's disliked. No. He was denied full access to the electorate; he was not permitted to make himself fully understood. The press was hostile and his opponent spread outrageous lies and falsified issues. Even if he wins, a small voice wonders about those who voted the other way. Why did they do that? Why did they reject me? This is the small voice in the heart of every politician which says that if there were money enough and time to reach every voter the result might be . . . unanimous. It is absurd on its face, to invest so much with the promise of so little. Except one is impregnated with history, true and false. The ghost of Lincoln hangs over the shoulder of every serious American politician. To console a nation! "To free from the sense of misery." One conceives oneself suspended in an ineffable state of melancholy, balanced between the truths of Freud and Lincoln. Is it not necessary therefore to find a code of conduct that will not slander either side, or defame oneself?

Honor, power, riches, fame, and the love of women—my press secretary and I call it the hots. That's the moment in a speech when the words begin to burn and the audience moves in close, feeling the rhythm. A passionate speech requires a passionate audience. It can happen at any time, anywhere, but usually it happens at a rally, when you're preaching to the converted. Shirt sleeves up, you throw away the text and give it to them hard, aiming low. You step out from behind the podium, reaching, no barriers between you and them, and beat time to the music. You are one with them and the energy is *felt,* flowing both ways, a reciprocal current. It happens only a few times in any campaign.

The first time I ever saw it was in 1966, my first run for the House. Robert F. Kennedy, then the junior senator, came up to help me out. It was a hot day in early October; we rode in a motorcade from the airport to the civic center for a rally. The crowds were enormous and downtown the motorcade slowed to a crawl. The senator ordered the car stopped and grabbed a portable bullhorn and stood on the hood and shouted an impromptu speech. He filled the air with fire and wit, drawing cheers and laughter at the same time. Sweating, roaring into the bullhorn, he created a prizefight atmosphere. This was fifteen rounds, he was the world champion, and I was the protégé. *Give me some help down there!* he cried. *The nation needs Tom Lewis! We've got to have him!* Then he began to laugh out loud. *Only Tom and I can save the republic from Republicans! Isn't that what you want? Only Tom and I stand between you and the party of Harding, Hoover, and Nixon!*

It was outrageous and the crowd loved it, roaring back its approval. Kennedy waved his muscular arms and the crowd waved back. I knew then that I would not lose, and when he got back in the car, smiling happily, flushed, I told him excitedly that he'd done it; the campaign was won. He shrugged and turned away, reaching to shake someone's hand. Hands were everywhere around us. He said that one speech didn't make a campaign. That one did, I said. I groped for words, It was electric, high-voltage. He smiled mischievously. "It isn't electric," he said quietly. "Electricity has nothing to do with it. It's sexual."

My opponent never recovered from that day, unseasonably warm, in early October. I believe that if our elections were held on the first Tuesday in September, our politics would be transformed. August would be the decisive month. The August heat would demand an altogether different style. In the August heat Nixon never would have been elected. I've never seen him in shirt sleeves in a fairground or union hall; he had no idea how to work a crowd in the heat. No idea what to do with the hots if he had them. But our elections are not in September, they are

in November. One suits one's style to the seasons. Of course it is
necessary to be in tune, to understand the nature of the dreams and
nightmares of the population. That is something that has preoccupied
me for twenty years, since Bloomington. The apparatus of control is
fragile, and the people require consolation.

I worked for a congressman for ten years, first as intern and then as his
legislative assistant and finally his administrative assistant, and when he
retired I ran to succeed him and won. It was an arranged retirement.
He supported me and that (along with Senator Kennedy) made the
difference, and even today I consult him on serious political matters
relating to the district. He knows all the closets and all the skeletons in
them; a great man for detail. I am entirely secure now, the last time out
I had no opposition at all. (My victory may be said to have been
unanimous.)

Since my election, my wife and our two children live in the district,
in the house she grew up in; her father, my predecessor and patron the
congressman, lives down the street. The house, his house, was his present to us the year I ran for his seat and won. It is a large Victorian house
in a neighborhood of other large Victorian houses. Weekdays I live alone
in a small apartment near the Capitol. I am home virtually every weekend, so that is in no way a hardship. My weekends home follow a
predictable pattern: I arrive Friday night, hold open house in my office
on Saturday morning, visit friends on Saturday night, and on Sunday we
all have lunch with my in-laws. His health is not good, and I believe that
in his heart of hearts he wishes he were back on the Hill. Gail and her
mother cook and the old man and I talk politics. I ask his advice on
legislation and then I bring him up to date on all the congressional
gossip, particularly that relating to his old friends. George Davies was
a particular kind of Washington legislator, a figure more of the last
century than of this one. His weekends were spent in the Library of
Congress, and his fund of Washington knowledge was prodigious. He
could name the artist who drew the two murals in the Lincoln Memorial

(Jules Guérin), describe with quick wit the decades of quarreling that delayed the construction of the Washington Monument, and digress for hours on the contradictions of the American political system. In other words, a proper Washington bore, but a bore with style, and I remain very fond of him. This family, her family, is now mine as well. I feel closer to my father-in-law than I ever did to my own father, though we are very different men. He is extremely shrewd, an old man who knows what he wants.

I like living alone in Washington. My apartment is pleasant and not expensive, and quite private when I have guests. I have a hideaway office in the Capitol building itself to which I return nearly every evening after dinner. I love the old big-domed building, echoing at night, with its marble floors and pompous statuary and distinctive aroma; it is a government aroma, the damp smell of old paper and tobacco. Or, as a friend of mine puts it, "the smell of drift and inaction." I have never bothered to learn anything about the building, its length or its height or the identities of the architects. Those are the sort of facts that fascinate my father-in-law, and the other senior men. I am interested only in the effects, the largeness of the chambers, the pomposity of the design, and the silence at night. It is a comfortable building if you belong to it, and overwhelming if you don't. Those of us who work after hours in the Capitol building form a kind of fraternity. It's a fraternity of inside men who know and respect each other regardless of party; a thoroughly masculine world.

I'll have dinner and return to the office and work for two hours on correspondence and legislation and then prepare a stiff scotch and sit at my desk, feet up, and meditate. My office in the Rayburn Building is ceremonial, photographs and flags and certificates of one kind and another. The hideaway office is for work only, except for a small bookshelf containing the New York edition of Henry James. That is a legacy from my past, but a legacy that is always with me. I have read all the novels and short stories and Leon Edel's biography, and I regard the master as an old friend. I freely concede that this is odd; the world of Henry James is miles away from mine. However, the atmosphere in Washington has been rancid for years; to be precise, for ten years, from the moment I became a congressman. It will take a generation to cleanse it. I live and work in Washington and do not feel obliged to read about it in novels. I expect I am somewhat disappointed and stale, and in that I reflect the city. At any event I prefer the Europe of Henry James and I connect with his rhythms: he writes of ordinary men in extreme situations.

I have not read any of his books lately because I have been studying my "image." The assistant majority leader is due to retire this year and there has been some speculation that I'll be put forward to succeed him. There is no obvious candidate and the leadership is determined to avoid a brawl. We are trying to prepare the battlefield from behind the scenes. I won't get the job because I'm too junior, but I'll work to get it, though in the circumstances there's a limit to what a man can do for himself.

The image is this. Hardworking Tom Lewis. Thomas Giles Lewis, forty-four, a ten-year veteran of the House, strong with the unions, respected by businessmen, moderate-liberal. No firebrand as an orator, but in the House of Representatives that's evidence of maturity. "His name is attached to no specific piece of legislation, but scores of bills over the years bear his fingerprints." A family man, well liked on both sides of the aisle. "Clean." The shrewdest of the reporters wrote that "his commitment to the House is genuine. He seems to lead two lives, one in Washington and the other with his family in the district, and he appears to be uncommonly successful at it." I would say middling successful, but then I'm a party at interest. Reporters, so secure in the cocoon of their professional neutrality, are especially fond of the word "commitment." They do not appreciate the double meaning. (Reporters are like Germans: they are either at your feet or at your throat.)

The image is accurate in all important respects. I do a politician's work and am paid for it and am obliged to defend myself and my record every two years, which is more than I can say for newspaper reporters.

Still, I am bemused—perplexed, perhaps—by the image, the grand march of verified facts. Legislation supported and opposed; issues joined or avoided; men defended or abandoned. This C.V. discloses quite a lot: quite enough for a voter to make an informed judgment.

These thoughts are common among politicians, narcissists all. We scorn the image one moment and embrace it the next. But it is always with us, a shadow variously cast, a permanent doppelgänger. The night I thought seriously about my image I also thought seriously about Dement. Brother Warren had made a new offer, the most generous yet; my lawyer urged me to accept. I sat in the hideaway until midnight, drinking scotch and doodling on a yellow pad and thinking about my image, the leadership, Dement, and the various women I had known. My mind roamed among the four. What would it be like to dispose of Dement? My third interest in an insurance agency? At midnight I decided to call Gail. The telephone rang half a dozen times before she answered, groggy and irritated at being awakened. We talked a moment of this and that, how she was, how the children were, how I was, how her parents were. Then there was silence between us.

I have always hated the telephone, an unfortunate circumstance because I'm on it about two hours a day. I like to watch people when I'm talking to them. Faces disclose more than words, and now I tried to visualize Gail lying in bed, her head buried in the pillow, the telephone receiver held askew to one ear.

She said, "Where are you now?"

"I'm in the hideaway."

"It sounded like it, your voice is always friendlier when you're there rather than the Rayburn. What are you doing there at this hour?"

"Working. Having a drink."

"You don't sound like you're drinking," she said.

"And thinking," I said. I suddenly thought of my father. What would he have to say about my political career? What would be his advice? He would say, without doubt, "Slow down." Those would be his first words to me. The next two words would be, "Watch out."

"Anything new?" She meant with the retirement of the assistant leader. I said there wasn't. She said, "When will you know?"

I pictured her in the second-floor bedroom, her night-light on, puzzled by this call. I said, "A couple of weeks. They're sorting it out now. It'll take time." She yawned and smothered the yawn with a giggle. I said, "I'm going to Dement at the end of the week," and listened carefully for her reply.

"Dement?" She was silent a moment. "Tom, I don't want to go to Dement."

I said, "I'd like you there."

"Well, why? I've never gone before. You've always gone to Dement alone."

"I'm going to accept the latest offer. It's a pile of money and I'm going to take it and run. Sell my share of the agency, and cut that cord at last. It could be embarrassing, having an interest in an insurance agency." That was only half true. "It would be a help to me if you were there. I'd appreciate it, Gail. Really."

"Tom, it's impossible."

I said, "Two days. Thursday and Friday."

She was not happy and listed the things she had to do before the weekend. It was a long list. "I'm sorry, I'd like to. But it's too much."

I said mildly, "Shit." I knew I could persuade her.

"I *am* sorry," she said. "Go to bed now."

But I didn't. I hung up the telephone and sat silently for another hour. I made a fresh drink and reflected that the largest decisions were often made in the most casual ways. One way or another I had been associated with the agency all my life. But it was time to move along now.

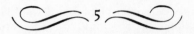

My wife and I were married two years after I went to work for her father. She had gone to George Washington University and then worked for a congressman from Indiana, her godfather, in fact. (As later the congressman's son would work for *her* father.) We fell in love right away, almost the day we met, which was a month after I went to work in her father's office. The courtship was smooth, though she kept delaying the wedding date. She said there was no hurry, and of course there wasn't. But she anticipated problems between me and her father.

I was fascinated by the centeredness and continuity of her life. She was a true Washingtonian, though she'd not actually grown up in the city; she'd lived with her mother in the district in upstate New York. But her father had been in Congress for twenty years and he shared everything with her. He and her mother kept their distance; she was the link between them. It was a congressional family, the old man consumed by his work; table talk between him and his daughter concerned politics and little else. She had a profound sense of the town, though for her it was always The Capital, pronounced Warshinton. Perhaps she took it too seriously. She said she would never live there as the wife of an elected official. Her words: Elected Official. Her parents' arrangement was ideal. She would prefer not to live in Warshinton at all, but to live "at home," as her mother did. Warshinton was a transient town of shifting alliances. There was too much movement and commotion, and while she understood it, and loved living there as a single person, she did not want to be on the premises as a congressional wife. Any more than her mother had been.

Of course I wanted very badly to be an "elected official," and the two years of our courtship were thick with discussion and argument about *where.* Dement was out of the question. I did not care to pursue a political career or any kind of career in Dement or anywhere else in Illinois. It was the Congress I wanted. I wanted to be one of four hundred and thirty-five *congressmen.* Why? Perhaps I felt there was safety in numbers. But I did not believe it would ever happen. The House seemed unattainable to me. Elective office was surely beyond my grasp, I had no money and no "base" and no proven ability. Eventually I put "elected official" in the back of my mind and began actively to cast around for something else. I was at loose ends in all ways, believing the prize forever beyond me. Meanwhile, I picked away at my job, A.D.C. to a father-in-law. I knew it would not last. A year after Gail and I were married it became clear to me that he had plans. Without any formal agreement between us it was understood that I would be his successor. The timetable would be of his own choosing. But increasingly I would accompany him on trips back to the district, occasionally filling in for him at a Rotary Club lunch or a Chamber of Commerce dinner. These appearances were successful. Each year he delegated more of his authority, but no one was more surprised than I when, in 1964, he told me he would announce his retirement early in 1966. I would have to fight a tough primary, but if I was energetic "we would win." I would win with his help. My father-in-law was a man of the old school, and I had not worked for him for ten years and lived with his daughter for eight without knowing how his mind worked. I knew there would be a condition and I waited for him to spell it out.

"Give her up," he said.

We were sitting in his office. It was late at night and no one else was around. I flushed, muttered something, and looked away. His words were not angry and they carried no hint of threat, but he was not pleading either. He had advanced a simple statement of fact.

"That's the quid for the quo."

"Hell, George," I began.

"No, that's what it is. And not tomorrow and not next week. Right now. Tonight."

"She's just a friend," I said.

He smiled. "Then it ought to be easy."

"Well, it won't be easy."

"Call it what you want. I don't want to hear any details. I know most of them anyway. That's the bargain."

I was silent for a moment. He leaned back in his desk chair, staring at the ceiling. Then he lit a cigar, rolling the tip in the match flame. He pushed the cigar box across the table but I shook my head.

"You know I love Gail," I said.

He looked at me sharply. "We'll leave Gail out of it."

"I just meant—"

"I know what you meant," he said.

My mind was racing. "It isn't what you think. I don't know what you've heard." I said, "This town is full of gossip. You know how this town is, you have a friendship—" I said, "Anything is open to misinterpretation, but I certainly—" Then I looked at his face and I knew I had made a mistake. George Davies was not a fool and did not like to be taken for one. I moved my hand as if to erase the words from the air. He looked at me and nodded slowly. Then he leaned across the table and spoke directly, his words cold as frost. He said he wasn't interested in morals, mine or his. He was not a priest, he was a politician; and he was a father and grandfather. He knew there was nothing he could do for the long term, but he had an obligation to his family. If in two years I decided to renew this . . . friendship . . . there was nothing he could do about it. But he was betting that wouldn't happen. He said, "I've watched you closely. You're smart, you're loyal. You are going to make an excellent member of this House. You can go as far as you want to—"

"With your help," I said.

He nodded. "With my help." He said it was a business arrangement. It was an entirely private transaction and I could accept it or not, as I chose. That was my business. But he would expect an answer first thing in the morning. A *fait accompli,* one way or another. He said, "You think it over." Then he looked at his watch, put on his hat, said good night, and left the office. I sat stiffly in the visitor's chair, his cigar smoke all around me, and listened to the door close and his footsteps retreat down the marble corridor. Then I called Jo and told her I would be there for dinner as planned.

Gail was visiting her mother in the district. In those days she went back for a long weekend once a month, and it was during one of those absences that I'd met Jo. We were introduced at a crowded cocktail party; our host described me vaguely as someone who worked on the Hill. She asked me what I did on the Hill. I told her in as few words as possible, and understood after a moment that she had no idea what "the Hill" was. She lived entirely apart from political Washington, then and later. She listened to me politely, nodding and asking what she hoped were the right questions. I said finally, "You don't give a damn about any of this, do you?" She shook her head. No, she really didn't. I said, "Does the phrase 'House Ways and Means' mean anything to you?" No, she said. Sorry, it doesn't mean anything at all. Then, smiling: "I really didn't understand much of what you were saying a minute ago. I gather you work for a congressman. What do you do for him?"

"Legislation," I said. "And political business back in the district." She nodded, apparently satisfied. I said, "The congressman is my father-in-law."

She said, "Your poor wife."

I was startled. "Say again," I said.

"It must be awkward for her."

"Why would it be awkward?"

She looked at me strangely. "Well, what happens when there's an argument? Whose side is she supposed to be on? She's sure to offend someone, no matter what she says. Your poor wife, she's walking through a minefield."

"We don't argue," I said.

"Not at all?"

"Well, it's the office. It's business—"

She laughed and touched my arm. "Passing strange. That's all I ever did. Argue with my mother-in-law. We could make an argument out of anything, the weather, sex, religion, the competence of clerks at Marshall Field's—" She explained that she and her husband were separated. He was a lawyer in Chicago, she'd come to Washington because she had friends here. She sculpted; in fact she had a show at one of the local galleries. She reached into her purse and fished out a business card and handed it to me. It was the address of a gallery near Dupont Circle. Come tomorrow at five, she said. If you can stand bad sherry and the local art mob. Then she shook my hand and was gone.

I arranged to stop by the gallery the next day. Of course, I knew no one there and was ill at ease until she took me in hand and explained what it was she was doing with her sculpture. It made as much sense to me as my explanations of the Hill did to her. Her pieces were constructed in papier-mâché and were circular and all of them were white. The walls and ceilings of the gallery were white and the effect was disorienting, her white globes against the white walls. Each globe had a piece cut out of its skin, revealing the interior. In some extraordinary way the globes seemed reflective of her. I did not understand what she was doing but I knew it was genuine.

I took her to dinner that night and told her I had once contemplated becoming an artist. She smiled; I think she thought that artists were born and not made. They did not, in any case, "become." She asked me why I didn't. I said I believed there were inside men and outside men and I was an outside man. "Except professionally. Professionally, I'm an inside man."

"That's very clear. I'll remember that always."

I was laughing. "I knew you'd find it helpful," I said.

"Actually," she said, "I do understand what you mean. I'm a little surprised that I do. But I do."

I found myself reminiscing about the Midwest, Dement, and my father's campaign for lieutenant governor. I found I had near-total recall, the memories clear and sharp and funny. I could not stop talking, it was as if a door in my mind had swung open. "Let me tell you about Freud's Twenty-third Psalm." I embarked on a comic fantasy, connect-

ing the episodes of my life to her papier-mâché globes: plunging through
the diverse entrances to the empty spaces within, all the empty quarters
of my mind. I loved making her laugh.

"They're not empty," she said.

"Unexplored," I said. "A wadi of the mind."

"No, no," she said urgently. "That's a mistake. The shape of the
space defines it. That's what it *is*. Put in there what you want to, it's
the shape that matters. That's what you have to know in your heart. The
dream fits the shape." She was using her hands now, cupping them,
describing arcs; I watched her, enchanted. I nodded gravely, then
laughed. "That one of yours, the globe near the door? The shape of that
one, perfectly seamless and nothing within. Hate to tell you, but it looks
like Wilbur Mills."

"Inside or outside?"

I thought a minute. "Both ways."

She grinned happily. "Tommy," she said. "Who is Wilbur Mills?"

"A powerful chairman," I said.

"Like Mao?"

I laughed. "There is no difference between them at all," I said.

We became lovers that night. I remember walking to her house
from the restaurant, holding hands, walking head to head, our shoulders
touching, ducking into a dark doorway, then resuming course. Her house
was a revelation to me. An empty birdcage hung from the ceiling of the
living room and reproductions of the Baroque portraitists decorated the
walls. There were no rugs and very few pieces of furniture and the effect
of the space was austere, though wonderfully softened by the portraits
—a melancholy prince, a soldier, a young woman in repose. Our footsteps echoed on the hardwood floors. Thick cushions were scattered here
and there. A full bookcase and a tiny white player piano sat side by side.
One of her globes rested in front of the fireplace, the center of attention.
Fresh flowers were on the mantel. I felt I had known the room all my
life and was just returning to it, although the objects in it were foreign
to me. She put a record on an old red Webcor and drew the curtains

and opened a bottle of wine. Then she looked at me, smiling shyly. "It's all right, isn't it." She meant the room and it was a statement, not a question. She said, "It's mine."

There was a month of craziness, a high-wire act of late-night telephone calls and telegrams, two letters a day, clandestine meetings in road-houses, afternoons in motels, arranged encounters in art galleries, and one weekend in New York. From the beginning we agreed it was a lunatic affair and would have to end. We had no future, our lives were different, and there were many too many complications. I was a married man, etcetera, and she was a woman of character, etcetera. But I did not truly believe it. When we were together excitement carried us along and all doubts vanished. I was spellbound by the moment, ignoring the precariousness of the affair; I believed that somehow it would solve itself. I refused to think beyond the moment, unwilling to disturb in any way what we had found together.

At the end of the month I had to visit the district on business and when I returned she was beside herself. She said she could not continue. She said she was incapable of maintaining a frenzy. There was enough frenzy in her work, she did not need it in her life. It was all wonderful but insupportable. Her life did not work in that way. She couldn't sculpt and was worried all the time and was being driven out of her mind by guilt. This was an entirely different Jo. I tried to joke and jolly her out of it, I was so happy to see her again I did not listen carefully. But her mind was made up. She was firm: this was it. I did not understand what "it" was. I said I couldn't bear to be without her, not to have her in my life in some way; if that was what she wanted, I'd leave Gail. Gail and my work were part of another life altogether. No, she said; she couldn't bear that either, not yet anyway. But that was my own decision and she did not want to be a part of it. She said, Leave me out of that. She was miserable because she didn't know what to do. What were the choices? Always before there had been choices. This was a problem with no solution. But something had to change.

Jo said, "You. You've got to figure something out."

"I will," I promised. I was eager for responsibility. I would take charge and devise a strategy.

"Now. Right now."

"All right," I said and kissed her. I had no ideas at all.

She smiled sadly. "Because I am going nuts."

We spent a fortnight apart and I considered the possibilities. I was not thinking clearly because it had all happened so fast, and was so new to me. I was unchained for the first time in my life, amused and delighted in spite of the dilemma. I meditated, listening for echoes; I heard clamor. I am cautious by nature: I do not move quickly. I am accustomed to delay and obfuscation. I have learned that often the best and wisest course is to do nothing and wait for a harmonious solution to present itself. I believe the only way to control events is to let them play, intervening at the decisive moment. But the forces at work must be seen clearly and all I saw was a warm and amorphous haze. Nothing in my life had prepared me for this. I felt my own compass swing on its axis and was content to let it swing. I felt my chains snap, and fall away.

It was exhilarating: whatever happened, life would never be the same. One's vision was forever altered and enlarged. Forever there would be dates remembered, specific times and places that would be with one always, memory's shadow. A life had changed direction. I believed there was no obvious way to "play" it; it was a throw of the dice —Einstein's random universe, perilous and unpredictable. I knew that Jo was obliged to see it differently. Jo loved complication, her life was a series of conscious choices. But the risks were not hers, they were mine. I explained that to her and she smiled (not unkindly), replying: "You have no idea of the risks that women take."

She listened very carefully. I said what men always say. I explained that I would need time, perhaps six months' time; there were practical considerations. . . .

Saying nothing for a moment, her face a mask, she then began to talk about her work. There were now two things in her life, me and her work. I had to understand that they were . . . "poised." She said, "I would not give up my work in order to have you. I would not give you up in order to have my work. It is not a comfortable place for me, but there it is. I'm on a knife's edge and I wish it were different but it isn't." She paused, struggling with the words. "You cannot expect too much from me in this. It is really your play. *But I will not be toyed with.*" She gestured at one of the globes. "Do you know how long I've studied and how hard I've worked in order to reach the point where I can create that? I have been working at it for fifteen years, fighting everyone. . . . I don't know yet what you hang on to. That's what I hang on to. That's the visible effect of my life." All of this was said very slowly and seriously. "I do not mean to be anyone's creature. I did that once and it didn't work out. How can I explain this to you? I do not put my work first. But I don't put it second, either. The two, you and my work, are equals. And separate—"

I said, "In balance."

She nodded. "Yes. I don't talk about it much, except to you. Men are not conditioned to take a woman's work entirely seriously, no matter what it is. In their tour through the maze that's a fact that's neglected. Sad but true."

"Nonsense," I said.

"No," she said. "It's not nonsense."

We talked most of the night, laughing often; the language of sex is laughter. We concluded we could meet once a month. In between times there were to be no telephone calls and no letters and no (she was smiling) telegrams. The telegrams, she loved those most of all. She had them all, plus the letters, in a shoe box. Yes, she said finally, of course we can try it. Perhaps it'll even work for a while. But no more daily frenzy. She couldn't eat or sleep but most of all she couldn't *work*. I agreed to all conditions (my own work had never gone better). Of course she was right, but I loved the commotion and excitement and abandon of it, life running at full tilt. I had never had that before. I described it exactly as I felt it, the words tumbling over themselves.

"I understand," she said gently.

"Really?" I was pacing up and down in front of her.

"Really. It's the same with me." Then she smiled, amusement finally bubbling over. "Except that it's different."

I moved to the window and stood looking into the empty street below. Soft early-morning light had slipped in unnoticed. Across the street a man in a dressing gown appeared on his front stoop and picked up the newspaper, unfolding it and glancing quickly at the headlines on page one. His expression was grave; this was the first news of the day, negotiable currency for today's transactions. I had to smile, it was so familiar: a Washingtonian and his morning newspaper. The man in the dressing gown seemed completely unaware of his surroundings. He peered at page one and grimaced. Then he turned abruptly and walked back into his house, closing the door smartly behind him.

The street was empty again but I continued to look into it, diverted by the long line of spare, monotonous, Federal facades. This was a very old and formal part of Georgetown. Two-hundred-year-old eagles crouched fiercely in horseshoe arches above lacquered doors, the eagles wrapped in Old Glory. I thought it an odd district for an artist to live in.

I heard her voice from the bed. "I couldn't continue living on a string, even when I know you're at the other end. People can't live like that." She smiled, her mouth turning down at the corners. "Doing themselves no favors. *I* can't."

I was avoiding the hard question. "I really believe we are one. One heart, one soul. I've believed it from the first—"

"No, baby," she said. "We are not one. We are two." She said, "Sometimes we are one. We are one sometimes when we are together and occasionally when we are apart and thinking the same thoughts. Otherwise, at those other times, we are two. Two persons. Separate." She looked hard at me, wanting to continue.

I continued for her. "And sometimes I am with someone else."

"Bravo," she said.

I corrected myself. "Most of the time."

She nodded slowly, wanting it understood.

I looked at her. "And that is intolerable."

She shook her head no. No, not intolerable. "But it doesn't make us one, either."

In that way the six months became a year, and the year became eighteen months.

I left the congressman's office that night-of-the-ultimatum and drove slowly down Pennsylvania Avenue to M Street and then up to Prospect, where she lived. I was thinking of her, not what I would have to say to her, but of *her.* Jo laughing with her mouth turned down and her head cocked, a lock of auburn hair curling over one eye, her fingers describing arcs in the air; Jo in her shapeless sculptor's smock and black tights, explaining that she had a stepfather who had a stepfather. She called her stepfather "Step" and her stepfather's stepfather "Step-step." Her laugh, low and subtle and suggestive; her anger, her turbulence, her unexpected passion. She was now as much a part of my life as my eyes and ears. I told her once that she was my sixth sense; that if we were ever separated for any reason I would return like a transmigrated soul to my former state, insurance man in Dement, Illinois. I would be just like everyone else, and so would she. There would be nothing unique about us at all.

She'd said to me once, "I can see into you. The part I love is on the inside. I don't understand the outside. In some odd way I think you're miscast. What is on the inside doesn't agree with what's on the outside. I cannot see you as a representative of anything. You are real to me only when you're here, in this house. I saw you the other night on television. Some congressional thing, it was just a glimpse and I couldn't connect with it. With you. I thought, Here is the man who shares my bed and all the thoughts I have. A man I dream with, a cheerful man who laughs with me naked in bed. This other man is a serious man in a white shirt and a blue suit. Not the same man at all,

I said to myself. Then I started to cry and I cried on and off all night. Not for me. For you."

We almost never talked politics at her house, though from time to time she'd ask me to explain something she'd read in the newspapers. She would listen to my explanation and shake her head, bemused. Occasionally her indifference would irritate me. But of course that was part of the attraction. Sometimes I talked about one of my current projects whether she wanted to hear about it or not. She was always polite but I knew her mind was elsewhere. Only once did I fully engage her interest, and that was when I told her about the hots, which was then only an idea and not a fact of my life. She said she understood that all right. How many people went into politics because of the hots? Not too many men, I said. Most men went in for reasons of personal ambition, meaning power, money, and fame. I didn't know about the women; I'd always assumed with women that politics was a substitute for something else. What about you? she asked me. I said I wasn't sure, I'd have to campaign first; I suspected that it would be the hots, but I wouldn't know for certain until I'd done it. But I knew I wanted to be a representative, an outside man.

I wish now that I had told her more about my professional life, what I did during the daylight hours. I mean details. But our life together was grounded in a different world, an interior nighttime world that was closed to the outside. She had no doubts whatsoever that I would get what I wanted. She said, "It'll happen. It'll happen for sure. It's the way you've defined your space, or had it defined for you. I suspect your family defined it. Anyway, it's a compulsion. You're like a speculator plunging to protect his investment."

I'd said, "Don't I have anything to say about it?"

I remember her low laugh. "Don't you wish you did?"

"Well, you're in the same situation."

She looked at me sharply. "No. I arise from disorder. You arise from order."

I said, "The result is the same."

She lifted her shoulders, a noncommittal comment. She said, "You can't imagine my life."

I said, "I know your work well enough. It's singular. Your own creation."

She smiled at that. "Yes," she said softly.

How I loved to watch her work: I'd curl up in a chair and read and she'd sculpt, talking to herself, complaining, exhorting, criticizing, humming music, occasionally looking at me, reciting odd bits of poetry. I'd listen to the performance and then become attracted to the black tights she wore when sculpting. We made love in the afternoon, listening to Vivaldi, *Four Seasons,* the summer movement. It was there in her studio on Saturday afternoons that I discovered Henry James. On Saturday afternoons in the house on Prospect Street the books fit perfectly with the music, my mood, the white globes and black tights, the warmth and serenity of the room and her vivid presence.

I drove to Prospect Street, parked in the alley, and let myself in through the back door. She was upstairs and called down: she was on the telephone, she'd be a minute. *My mother,* she whispered hoarsely. I made a drink and leaned wearily against the sideboard. I had avoided thinking about the congressman, but all that came back now with a rush. I could hear his careful voice and perfect sentences and his cigar smoke still clung to my suit. Then the memory ebbed. I stood very still, sipping my drink, staring into the blackness of her backyard garden. I could barely make out the crowded rosebush, the blossoms hanging like bells from a jester's costume. I switched off the kitchen light and the entire garden came alive in the moon. A night bird hammered noisily nearby, competing with the roar of a cocktail party two houses away.

Then she was in the room and I kissed her and we stayed together a long minute in the dark. She took my hand and led me into the living room. The curtains were drawn and the radio was on, turned very low. The empty birdcage swung on its axis. It was bright, four spotlights blazed from the ceiling. She said, "Look."

It was a new globe, this one was five feet in diameter.

"This is the new one?" She nodded. I looked sideways at her. "You're sure it's big enough?"

"Very funny, come here." She wanted me to see the opening. There were in fact two openings, one square and one rectangle; they seemed to be cut at random but I knew she'd worked out the size and placement on a slide rule.

I was stunned by it and muttered something admiring. I said quietly, "It's a breakthrough."

She said, "I think so." She was standing back from it, her knuckles to her chin, her elbow in the palm of her hand. Her face was glowing with pleasure. She leaned toward her creation as if she were taking a bow, running her fingers along the two openings, feeling the rough texture. "Feel that," she commanded. "You'll notice that it's concrete. In case you don't know it, that's hard to do. It's *very* hard to do. Many structural problems. But I love it and I'm really and truly happy with it." Then she laughed. "Of course, it may not be sold because it may never be moved. When they brought it here from downstairs they asked me if I'd take structural soundings. Of the *house.* They thought the house might collapse, clunk. It took four of them to move it. . . ." She laughed again, giddy with excitement.

"It's wonderful, Jo. It really is."

"Do you really like it?"

"I really like it," I said.

"Well anyway," she said. "It's new. It certainly is new."

"The size—" I began.

She nodded, "Yes."

"Why two openings?" I wanted to keep her talking.

She looked at me, bubbling over with excitement. "Oh, it's very symbolic. High symbolism." I laughed and she touched my arm, suddenly serious. "It was an idea. I'd never made two openings before. It's a whole new idea about space. It has no special meaning that I can understand. It's just that from the moment I started working on them, the openings, I knew it was right. They're where they ought to be." She moved around to the far side of the globe. "Look at it from this angle." I followed her. "And from this one." She got down on her knees, looking up. "And from down here, where you can just see the edges of both of them . . ." She paused, considering what she would say. "It's *correct,*" she said at last. "Whether or not it's successful, it's correct. Size and placement." She backed away from it now, her face set. "I want it shown in a room all by itself. A perfectly bare room, wood floors, bone-white walls. A fairly large room. I don't know yet whether the room should be square or rectangular. But the piece should be free-standing and located near a corner. People will have to *approach* it, as if it were a sovereign. As people come closer to the globe they should become almost hypnotized until as they get very near they will cease to see anything else and will contemplate *it* only. They will become one with the whiteness and the roundness. If they are looking at it properly, they will imagine the openings begin to expand and spread like an eclipse of the sun. Expand and expand until of course there is nothing at all. They are left with an idea of an idea: the opening becoming the thing itself. If they're *really* looking at it, it'll be an overwhelming experience. They'll never forget it, it'll be in their memories forever, staying with them, the fondest memory they have, a memory as vivid as something special recalled from childhood or earlier. It's a celebration of possibilities. Infinite possibilities, no limits on what can be attempted or achieved." She paused and smiled broadly, consciously breaking the spell.

I was shaken. It was the most direct and explicit she'd ever been. A celebration, she'd said. I said nothing, my mind was racing over her words. She took my hand and squeezed it.

"That is, if I can ever get it out of here in one piece. If it can be moved." She was racing for cover now. "I'm going to put a good fat price on it."

I let her go. I said, "You ought to. No price is high enough." I thought, No price was high enough for her. I nudged her. "A breakthrough piece demands a breakthrough price."

"Five thou," she said. "How much is that in francs?"

"I don't know. I think it's twenty-five thousand francs."

"Well, twenty-five thousand francs, then."

"Why francs?"

She turned away from me. "Because they've offered me a show in Paris."

I took her by the shoulders and massaged her gently. "That is sensational," I said.

"They asked me three weeks ago; it would mean I'd have to go for at least six weeks. And to tell you the truth, I want to go. For six weeks or longer. Making this thing has emptied me. I have poured myself into concrete and I feel a little crazy, that's to be honest with you. I want to go to Paris and go a little insane. With you. Maybe you could arrange it. We two—" She looked at me nervously, biting her lower lip. My heart turned over. "I pity anyone who has never been crazy in the soul." Then: "I've got to have all this stuff crated by next week, it's going over by ship and I'm going with it. But what about the new piece? It'll cost a fortune—" She giggled.

"Do it anyway," I said. "The hell with the cost, do it and up the price another five thousand . . . francs."

"Would you come?"

I retreated, moving my shoulders like a ballroom dancer, yes-no, maybe, perhaps, nothing's impossible in an uncertain world. I said, "It'll be hard."

"Oh, sure," she said. "But there are ways." She looked at me slyly. "I read something the other day about junkets. Isn't that what they're called? Congressional junkets at taxpayer expense?"

I laughed, she really was wonderful; she'd read one of the annual exposés in the newspaper. "Jo, that's the kind of thing that congressmen get defeated for."

"But you're not a congressman, you're staff."

I said, "I will be."

But she did not catch that. "Think of us in Paris. I'd have the show and we'd do the gallery drill, the opening and the stuff that goes with the opening. Parties, interviews. You could—"

"I could coach you on the interviews."

She smiled. "We'd hang around Paris. We'd fool around." She laughed out loud, imagining how it would be. "Then we'd go south. We'd take my winnings and just *go,* rent a car. We'd go south—"

I said, "The famous artist and her consort."

She looked at me. "Is that sarcasm?"

I looked back, surprised. "No," I said truthfully.

She moved away and cocked her head, pointing at the new creation. "I've got to call it something, it wants a name. . . ." She took my arm again. "This gallery in Paris, it's the best one, everyone says so." She stroked the globe again, unable to take her eyes off it. Its whiteness and haughty, regal roundness dominated the room, an imperial presence.

I wanted to get everything straight. "Why didn't you tell me before?"

"Well," she said stiffly. "We have our rules. We established our rules and I follow them. No calls, no letters or telegrams. And I wanted to make certain that it was sure, that it was locked up, this show. It's damn bad luck to *talk* it, you know. You can talk good news to death. At first I could hardly believe it, you know how pessimistic I am." She was silent a moment. "But mostly it was the rules. Our rules that we have established in order that we may live in some kind of orderliness without unwanted surprises." She looked at me eyes-on. "You know, save the whales."

She could always make me laugh. I said, "Jo."

"And I didn't know about you, whether you'd like it or not."

That hurt. "Honey," I said. "How could I not like it?"

She gave me the same look as before. "We'll be apart for longer than we ever have," she said. "Since this began. If you can't escape, and I suppose you can't. I suppose that isn't possible." She stopped talking and looked at me. "You won't, will you?"

I ignored the verb. "No," I said.

"Probably the most we'd have would be a week, ten days. For this particular celebration." She was looking out the window now, into the street, her face stretched into a smile; it resembled the formal mask of comedy. "Why not?"

That text was prepared. I thought, How can I? How can I disappear in Europe? There has to be an explanation for journeys abroad. Some explanation, however thin. I said simply, "It isn't possible." And I added, "For all the good reasons that you might imagine."

"Well, there's nothing to be done, then. It was such a good idea. I don't like to think about it."

"Neither do I." Just then I thought I had the first warning of her strategy, the manner in which she intended to stand in her own defense. She wanted precise bearings, nothing neglected. I wondered if we had each begun to take on the characteristics of the other.

She said, "Perhaps it's best. This is my business after all, there'll be quite a lot of business to be done in Paris. It isn't entirely pleasure, it's business as well. Business is separate. You said it once: one never argues about business." Her face was turned away from me. "Do you think it's best? I won't quarrel with you and I won't force you, but do you think it's best?"

I answered from instinct, "No." I looked at her and knew she understood. And I was wrong about the other, her characteristics were her own.

She said crisply, "I do." She turned off the overhead spotlights and suddenly we were in darkness. Her creation disappeared though its effects were still radiant. She said, "Come on, then." We walked back into the kitchen. It was perfectly still, the cocktail party nearby had ended. A dry breeze touched us through the open window. She was smiling her formal smile. We were both on soft surfaces, searching for a secure footing, trying to locate the high ground. She said, "That's out of the way now. We won't talk about it again. Make me a big drink, tell me about your day. . . ."

I relaxed, staring into the gray garden. I said, "Come on, you don't have to say that. You don't give a damn about my day." I was thinking about her show in Paris and what it would mean to her, and was dismantling my defenses as she was dismantling hers.

"I give a damn about you," she said. "You, your day. What's the difference?"

She knew better than that. But I was certain now that we were on safe ground and that there would be no ill treatment or malevolence. We approached the window together, as close in our emotions as that first night on the streets of Georgetown, but still we did not touch. "There is no difference between them at all," I said at last.

During those last minutes together I had forgotten absolutely about the *fait accompli.* I had not thought about that or about my wife and child or about my work. There were just the two of us and the life we had together, and the persistent avenging voice that told me this was a fresh turning and that she was obliged to go one way and I another. We had been together for more than a year and now we would have to be apart. What we had did not exist beyond the house on Prospect Street, it did not exist in Europe or New York City or any other place. We existed half-slave and half-free, and that was apparently the way we were meant to exist. It had worked, against all odds; but it would work no longer. To accompany her I would have to reject the others: not merely move away but consciously *reject.* I would have to tell them that they were not good enough for me, and that I would have to have this other.

I suddenly saw all the forces of my life with an awful clarity and knew the truth of the things she'd said. I had always thought of us as equals, "one," and abruptly we were no longer equals. We were what she had always claimed, "two people," "separate"—and everyone knew that separate was not equal. Except we had done such a good job, the casualties had been very light. I had always believed that casualties must accompany any good thing. The better the thing the higher the casualties. She'd said to me, *It's a celebration of possibilities . . . no limits on what can be achieved or attempted.* I knew that song intimately and I believed it was a solo; I knew it was. Standing at last in the garden, both silent, I was able to tell myself that I was no prize. Those words came very easily and of course were consoling. No doubt it was all for the best, you think you are so wonderful it's impossible for her to live without you; you think she'll collapse under the intolerable pressure of being alone or with someone else. Without your wise advice and tender counsel to guide her through her days. A minute or two of that was enough. The whales could not be saved. I believed that Paris would have taken us onto heights too high and vast and rarefied. We could not live there. I could not. I felt I had watched a gorgeous comet flash across the heavens, its sublime light immeasurably out of reach. But the comet was not her. It was us.

I called the next day. This was a breach in the agreement but we both knew the agreement was dead. It had expired and there was no renewing it. She said she would be leaving at the end of the week, not in two weeks as she had supposed. She'd spoken to her agent that morning and they were anxious to move along. The globe would go with her on the *France*, and it would be the centerpiece of the exhibit.

I did not want to leave unfinished business.

I said it would be a wonderful show.

"It would be fun sharing it."

I said, "More than fun. *Much* more than fun. Anyway, I'm there in spirit."

"D'accord to that."

I said, "Maybe you deserve this one alone."

She said slowly, "Maybe I do at that."

"A limelight," I said. I remembered her the first night in the gallery, patiently explaining about the globes, and later her agreement to have dinner. She chuckled and fell silent and I knew suddenly what it was that I wanted for her. Whatever it was she wanted for herself, that was what I wanted for her. I wanted an enormous success, something huge and tangible; acclamation from the demanding French. A sold-out show, a globe in the Louvre. I wanted it big, too big for her to handle right away; she needed a swelled head. I began to laugh. "I know what's in store," I said. "What you're going to get." I could feel her grinning along with me and my voice caught. "It's come to me in a hot flash. You'll get—honor, power, riches, fame, and the love of men."

"My God, all that?"

"Each one," I said. "At once."

"What about you, cornball? What do you get?"

"Me too," I said gently. "The same things. Exactly the same things."

I heard the breath go out of her. "Yes," she said.

There was dead air between us then. Neither of us dared speak. I watched a secretary's fingers skate over the keyboard of the typewriter, and the receptionist hand a document to a messenger.

I said finally, "I'll be campaigning." That was the unfinished business.

"Oh," she said. She began to talk about something else, then stopped. "You mean, you're going to run."

"Run like hell," I said.

"When did that happen?" Her voice slipped a little.

"You know when," I said. Then, "The old man is stepping down. I'll run next year but the groundwork begins now." She was silent, I could hear nothing over the telephone. "Jo?"

"Does Gail know?"

I stammered for a moment, struck dumb. She never mentioned Gail, ever. *"Does Gail know?"*

I said, "Her father may have told her."

She said, "You haven't spoken to her."

"No."

She said slowly, "I didn't feel like being the last one in on this particular bit of information. Now. What did it have to do with last night?"

"You're going to follow it all the way down, aren't you?"

She said, "Yes, I am."

"It didn't have anything to do with last night," I said. "It doesn't have anything to do with Paris." She began to reply but I rode over her words. "Nothing," I repeated. "Not anything."

"All right," she said.

"No, not all right. Not all *right.*"

"Gail didn't know?"

"No," I said. "And if she had, it wouldn't've made any difference."

She laughed quietly. "No difference at all."

I said, "None."

She said, "I'm going to name the globe after you."

I said, "I hope to hell."

"Tom," she said.

"It fits," I said, "and I'm honored." The buzzer sounded then, there was a quorum call on the floor. It was one of the amendments to a health care bill. The congressman emerged from his office and pointed at me, the gesture reminiscent of a baseball coach signaling the bullpen. He wanted me to come with him to the floor. I looked at the telephone receiver, winking at my father-in-law, indicating I would only be a moment.

"Best luck in the campaign," she said.

"Best luck in Paris."

She said, "Let me know what happens. Particularly—well, you know what particularly."

I said, "You too. The show. Tom."

"I will."

"Best luck in Paris," I said again.

She said, "Best love."

The congressman was standing impatiently at the door, jiggling the coins in his pocket. He looked at his watch, then at me again. He jerked his head: Come on.

I said, "Best love," and we hung up together.

Jo's show in Paris was a great success. The critics were unanimous in their praise, displaying both puzzlement and delight, an excellent combination in those times (and these). I sent her a long telegram the day the show opened and received a letter in return. She said it was fun to be a success in the City of Light. She remained there a month and then four more months and finally returned to Washington briefly to sell her house and collect her things and move back to Paris for keeps. We did not see each other; I was addressing a Rotary Club in the district.

But I kept my promise. The day after Kennedy came to campaign I cabled her in Paris. *Hots are real*, I said. *But periodic, like the atomic tables.* Then a paraphrase from Freud, *The way back from imagination to reality is art.* (The hots shepherd me, I shall not want.) I gave her a brief account of what Kennedy had said, and predicted that I would win the election. That was ten years ago, and the last I heard Jo was still in France, living quietly in the country with a French academic.

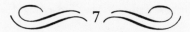

I flew into Dement in the early afternoon, beguiled as I always was by the flatness of the land, rectangular fields marching off to infinity. There was drought. The fields were various shades of gray, pockmarked here and there by oases of trees. Each field was plainly demarcated, as if it were a separate miniature nation; they were a thousand tiny nations in a vast dry continent. The city itself was triangular, its buildings low, its streets straight and even, curveless, fixed. The captain ordered us to extinguish all "smoking materials," and the de Havilland eased down, its engines sighing.

I looked for the family house but could not locate it among the trees, the hickories and maples and oaks. The town had grown in a year; Brother Warren had written me that it would be eighty thousand people before long. He said that once it was eighty thousand it would be no time at all before it was a hundred, if they could stop the rot downtown. If they couldn't stop it, they'd simply annex the surrounding countryside; the cat was skinned either way. Brother Warren spoke of a new golf course and three or four new restaurants and a new playing field for the high school. There was some talk about a community college but the city council could not agree on financing. Warren asked me were there any federal programs that Dement could plug into, payment on the come? Ask your congressman, I said. Lewis and Sons was prospering along with the town; it was now the largest insurance agency in a four-county area. Everyone was doing well and would continue to do well, if only the boom could be maintained.

I cinched my safety belt and the aircraft floated down, correcting its balance. The small field was clogged with private Cessnas and Pipers, and a few sailplanes. Skydiving and gliding had become quite the sports in Dement. A mile to our port side I watched a sailplane dip its nose and fall, gathering speed, then bank and rise, soaring beautifully. I wondered what my father would have thought of payment "on the come."

I turned to my wife, who was dozing, her head resting gently against the Plexiglas window. Her face was set; even in sleep she was facing the world stoically. I thought that she had gotten better-looking over the years. She did not look young, she looked exactly her age, forty-one, and she had put on weight, as I had. But she was a good-looking woman—now as then, except now she had character, a stamp, a mark as definite as an artist's brushstroke. I could recognize her in a crowd a hundred yards away, by the tilt of her head and her walk and the way her arms swung. I nudged her and she came awake blinking, her face still in repose. I asked her if any of it was familiar and she said it wasn't. Just the shape of the town in the middle of the fields, a triangular habitation. . . . It had been ten years since she'd accompanied me to Dement. She asked me who would meet us.

No one, I said. I'd told them I didn't know what plane we'd be on. I said I had political business in Chicago and didn't know when I'd get away. I'd let them know when we were settled at the hotel—except I intended to leave on the late commuter that evening. I wanted to avoid an overnight. There wouldn't be any hotel. I said to her, "I had an idea that we'd rent a car at the airport and have lunch together at a place I know."

She looked at me. "You seem almost happy."

"I am," I said.

"I always imagine you approaching Dement with dread."

"Do," I said.

"Well?"

"Well, this is different."

I collected a Chevrolet at the airport and we drove to the Wayside. My wife cautioned me twice; I always drive faster in the Midwest. I obeyed her warning the second time, just as I obey her instructions to have my hair cut, to make an appointment with the dentist, to have the car repaired, and to come to bed when it is late; she obeys me in similar matters. At other times we do not obey each other, though the warnings are spoken anyway. It was nearly two o'clock when we arrived at the restaurant and the parking lot contained only about a dozen cars. She looked at the building, whitewashed brick with a red tile roof and an enormous neon sign: STEAKS CHOPS SEAFOOD COCKTAILS. It had been years since I had heard a drink called a cocktail. She began to laugh, "This place, one of your poisonous roadhouses . . ." Her taste in food is more refined than mine.

I said, "A steak as thick as a gravestone, a baked potato the size of a shoe."

She said, "Good God!" Then, "I suppose you're going to have a martini."

I said, "Damn right. You, too."

She said, "I'll have a kir."

I shook my head. She would never get Dement right. I said, "The Wayside does not serve 'kirs.' They don't serve them even if you call them *blanc cassis.* You'd better have a martini, it will improve your disposition." I said, "You can have it on the rocks, clean." She made a face. "Or straight up. You can say, 'Silver bullet up, olive and twist.' "

She said, "Wonderful. How about a weak scotch? Do you think they can manage that?"

We were talking quietly in the foyer, waiting for the maître d' to seat us. I looked left into the bar and saw half a dozen men shooting dice for drinks. At the far end was a party of three women, their rugged heads close together, talking quietly. The women had apparently come from the golf course; they wore hats with golf tees stuck in the brims. Neither party seemed aware of the other, and the bartender stood poised midway between them. When the maître d' came he looked at me queerly, knowing he knew the face but unable to connect a name to it. When we were seated and he'd handed us menus I put out my hand. "Tom Lewis," I said. "Wife, Gail."

Well, *Tom,* he said. It had been too long. Four years, five. We chatted about the town and the weather. The growth and the drought. Then he left to fetch us drinks and when he returned we resumed the conversation. He said, "I suppose you're here for the dedication next week."

I shook my head. What dedication?

"Jesus Christ," the maître d' said. "Those brothers of yours. I suppose they were wanting to surprise you. A school is being dedicated to your father. Lewis School now, it used to be called South School. Remember?"

I remembered. A red brick building on a barren patch of land. A dusty baseball diamond and an iron jungle gym next to the ravine, and in the boys' room initials carved into the wooden partition between the toilets: TL.

"We all miss your father," he said, lowering his voice. "The one that's in there now." He shook his head. "No good. No damned good at all."

"Dead fifteen years next July," I said.

"Well, the firm has done real well." I nodded. "Your father would have been proud, all right. It's a fine thing, the school. You ought to go look at it, you couldn't recognize it. New addition." A customer on the other side of the room waved at him and jiggled his hand. The check. He turned to go.

"I'll look at it," I said.

My wife turned to me. "Did your father come in here often?"

"Sure," I said. "Every lunchtime for twenty years. Sat over there." I motioned toward a remote corner. "Had a schedule. He'd lunch with one friend on Monday and another on Tuesday. Always the same friends, same day of the week. Every week. Very orderly, my old man seemed to like that. Gave a shape to the week, he said."

She smiled. "You do the same thing."

"Correct," I said.

"It's funny, patterns in families. Fathers and sons and mothers and daughters."

I said, "This isn't a bad drink."

"I wonder if your grandfather did the same thing?"

"Yes," I said. "He did. Every day, except it was with his wife because he was a farmer—"

"And *his* father," she said. "I wonder if they were all in revolt against each other. Each following the same pattern—"

"It's so good I might have another."

"I wish I'd been a psychologist," she said suddenly. "That's really what interests me. I went to college and I had babies, that's what I did. And I was not a bad student. I could be working on the Hill now. That's where the serious work is being done," she said. "Social science, one or another of the soft sciences." She mentioned two pieces of pending legislation. "You know they had to farm out some of the research on that. There was no one on the committee staff capable of doing it, they didn't have the expertise—"

"Two more," I told a passing waiter.

We left the restaurant at three, my head buzzing from the drinks. I never drink at lunch, even a glass of beer makes me sleepy. We had an hour and a half to kill and I decided to take her on a short tour of the town. We went first to the house where I grew up, and then to the elementary school nearby—South School, now Lewis School. It was familiar to me but remote, the land around it less barren now; all of it was smaller than I had remembered. The neighborhood had not changed, but the school had a new steel and glass addition, with a square plaque to the left of the entrance: my father in bas-relief. He had been mayor the years I'd attended the school, a frequent speaker on Flag Day and Lincoln's Birthday and other national celebrations. The day the war in Europe ended he arrived breathless and called an impromptu assembly. I remember his first words: "We've licked the Axis." He led us in cheers and a brief prayer and the Pledge of Allegiance. Then he hurried off to perform the same rites at the other schools. But not before he'd dismissed us on "this historic occasion." We all rode downtown on our bicycles, to see what was happening; to see a historic occasion observed in Dement. But downtown was quiet, almost solemn; people were waiting for the end of the real war, the war in the Pacific. MacArthur's war.

The old schoolhouse was red brick and five stories high. I remembered how the wooden floors creaked, and the musty smell of the building, and the forbidding inner sanctum of the principal's office. School regulations were strict and authority and discipline absolute. Most of the teachers were spinsters and dry as old bones. There were only two men teachers; one taught shop and physical education and the other taught seventh grade.

The seventh-grade teacher had been wounded in the Pacific in the war, though none of the wounds was visible. At this time the war was still being fought, though no part of it seemed to touch Dement. This teacher, an ex-marine, was our only personal connection to the war. The class routines were in no way unusual, except the period devoted to arithmetic. He would carefully recite the lesson during the first half of the period and write questions concerning it on the blackboard. We were required to answer the questions during the second half. While we wrote he moved to the large windows overlooking the baseball diamond. The windows had shades with long black cords. He would take one of the cords in his fingers and begin to play with it, first twirling it like a lariat, then fashioning a noose, and finally tying knots in it, knot after knot, knot upon knot. It was a long cord and he was able to tie scores of knots, each building on the last until the cord was a hopeless tangle. We would watch him from our desks, bent over the oblong yellow work pads; alone of the teachers he required us to call him "sir," and in turn he addressed us by our last names, girls too. We watched him surreptitiously but he never turned around or acknowledged our presence in any way. The class remained very still, there were no disorders of any kind. He tied the knots and then untied them, his fingers working by feel alone; his hooded eyes were far away, staring into the playground, his expression blank. He finished untying the knots at precisely the moment the bell rang and would abandon the cord, leaving it dangling, kinked and gnarled and uneven, and would move to his desk to accept our papers silently. Then he would say "Class dismissed" in a thick voice and we would leave with a rush, anxious to be gone; it was the last class of the day. We would leave him at his desk with the papers.

He was at the school only one year, a small man with light wispy hair and china-blue eyes; he did not look the way we expected marines to look, even ex-marines. He had a face that was too small for his head. I remembered him vividly, standing in front of the window and staring into the playground, his fingers working by rote on the cord. God knows what his thoughts were. Of course he seemed very old and worn then, but he was probably in his early twenties, twenty years younger than I am now.

I'd parked in front of the school. I wondered what had happened to that seventh-grade teacher with the faraway eyes, where he had gone and what he did now. A casualty of war, I supposed; the school board determined that he was ill, unstrung, "not in control," and therefore unsuitable as a seventh-grade teacher. I heard it said that he was "not a good example." There was some commotion about it in the town but no one was prepared to cause trouble for the war effort, or embarrassment to the teacher. So he was fired quietly. To us at that time he was merely baffling, his behavior strange but never threatening; to my certain recollection, he never raised his voice.

"Do you remember his name?" Gail asked.

I said I had no idea.

"Poor man," she said.

I said, "They fired him."

She shook her head, angry. "I don't like this place at all."

"It's a small town like any other," I said.

"No it isn't," she said quickly.

I wanted to explain Dement to her, to find some way to convince her that the people there were no different from anywhere else. I meant, no meaner than anywhere else. It was simply that the norms were narrower, and perhaps that accounted for the dreams or fantasies of people like me; it was one way out. But it was unforgiving toward outsiders, no question of that; at times I was certain that the root of it was envy, at other times as convinced of the reverse.

She put her hand on my arm. "I didn't mean to be harsh," she said.

I smiled. "Not to worry."

"But it's so *closed,* so self-righteous—"

I shrugged, staring out the window at Lewis School, the plaque, the playground.

"—and as a matter of strict fact this place reminds me of her."

I stared at her, astonished. She never mentioned Jo, except one night years ago. We had talked about her in retrospect, calmly and rationally—too calm and too rational for either of us, but that was how it had gone. Later there were tears. I think we were both afraid of heat then; we did not know where that would lead us or with what result.

She said, "For years I thought it was a reaction to this place, here, where you had come from and what you'd been taught to expect. What you had been taught to believe was rightfully yours, or anyway *possible*. But you believed that passion came only in fantasy, not reality, and when the reality happened . . ." Her voice trailed away. Then, "I was not real to you. Maybe you thought she was the fantasy but she wasn't. I was." I began to reply but she interrupted. "That was the explanation that was easiest for me, that it was Dement and Dement's attitudes—you think you hated it, how do you think I felt? Feel. If it had not been for Dement there would have been no Jo. Jo would have happened long before, an extension of that other one. What was her name? It would not have been a threat that it took *my father* to solve. And that idiotic Freudian business, that was all tied up with Dement too. The one played off the other and the result was her." She put her hand to her mouth. "All those expectations and the means to fulfill them denied. Forbidden."

Gail lit a cigarette, exhaling in a rush. Ten years later the memory was still fresh, explicable now as it had not been that night. She smiled suddenly and I saw in her smile a flash of youth; Gail as she had been when I first met her. She said, "Of course I wanted to distribute blame. It was either Dement or it was me, and I was not eager to believe that it was me. Of course it could have been you, just you. You yourself. But I was not anxious to believe that, either."

I said, "It wasn't you."

She said, "Well, then." I put my arm around her shoulder but she did not yield right away. She was lost in her own painful memory.

"Look," I said, "I have what I want."

She looked at me. "All of them?"

I said, "All that I need."

She smiled then and I could see tears in the corners of her eyes. "You're not all that famous."

"I have plenty of honor."

"Or rich, either."

I laughed. "Will be, after today."

She turned away and ran her hand through her hair. She moved closer to me, though we did not touch. "And not very damn powerful, either."

"That leaves the last one," I said. "One to go."

She said, "I do not understand you at all, sometimes."

I said, "Stick to the strict facts."

"I mean to," she said.

"Come on," I said at last. "I'll show you the rest of the town." I put the car in gear and drove away. I do not remember everywhere we went that afternoon. I was on the west side of town, so I must have driven to the country club and the sprawling subdivision beyond. To the west the town gave way to farmers' fields, the fields decorated with billboards. I drove into the country a bit, then turned and headed back downtown. I was half asleep, driving slowly and cautiously through the unfamiliar streets. Then I was in the vicinity of the high school and made an abrupt turn to cruise by it. Where the Dement Township High School had been was now an apartment complex, and I remembered suddenly that five years ago it had been torn down and the land sold and a new consolidated school built closer to the center of population. I stopped the car and looked at the apartment building, another severe rectangle built (I supposed) with Title IV funds. I thought, Someone made a killing. Or no, not a killing; a massacre. I smiled; looking at this town gave the phrase "living off the land" new meaning. I knew that Lewis and Sons carried the insurance on the apartment complex, since Treasurer Bill was an early investor. The building, five years old, was already shabby and down-at-heel, and FOR RENT signs dotted the property. The old high school had been built like a fortress, it had taken months for them to demolish it. . . .

Well, I thought, it was not the Parthenon or even Lever House. All it had to commend it was a certain congruity with the town; it belonged. I remembered the governor in 1948, shy and hesitant in the gymnasium, groping for some vision he could lay before the hearts and minds of the citizens of Dement. I remembered the speech as a discussion of ideas and men, of the civilization that had resulted, and of the unquiet future. Ideas that had endured, men who had not. The importance of the land, fidelity to it; the beauty and challenge of the nation's principles, and fidelity to them. The gorgeous future, if. And the various threats of alien ideology. I remembered the restlessness and hostility of the audience; this was not a Chautauqua they enjoyed. It had occurred to them by then that land was no longer "the land" but "property," and that subversives were everywhere. They did not need to be lectured about their responsibilities, or promised bliss and ecstasy at some future political time. They wanted praise and reassurance now: not for what they did, but for what they were. To be told—what? That no sphinx would move in their lifetime. That the future was under control as long as they cleaved to what they were, and refused to budge. This one, striped-tied, who stood before them, so high-minded; he was an apostate, and could not be trusted.

I drove downtown and met with my brothers and my uncle and the two attorneys. It was very amicable; there were jokes. The attorneys conducted the final markup of the contract, speaking as if the principals were not in the room. They reviewed the contract line by line while the rest of us sat in silence, listening. Then each turned to his client and nodded. Everything was in order. All the conditions had been met, both men were satisfied. My brothers signed. I signed. Two secretaries signed as witnesses. A certified check was handed me by President Warren and I put it in my wallet without looking at it. Then we shook hands, strained smiles all around, and prepared to depart.

Warren said, "The *Trib* had an item about you the other day. Said you had a shot at the leadership of that place. A nice item, considering."

It always surprised me when any reference was made to my work by anyone in Dement. I said, "It's a long shot."

"I don't know how the hell you take it down there," Warren said. "Goddamn Washington." He shook his head as if to rid himself of a stubborn small pain. A man would have to be crazy to live in Washington, the muggers and the politicians and the bureaucrats, the filth. "Well," he said, "don't forget your friends and relatives."

I said, "Not a chance, Warren."

"Dad would've been proud."

I shook my head. " 'Fraid not. No, I think he held Washington in minimum high regard."

Gail looked at me and spoke for the first time. "Is that true?"

I laughed and said it was.

"Times do change," Warren said.

I said, "He wouldn't 've."

Warren grinned widely, eyebrows aloft; he looked more than ever like the old man. "It's the goddamnedest thing," he said. "When Dad was alive he wouldn't have anything to do with city insurance. You know, public buildings, casualty, fire, and so forth. Pension plans. No profit in it and a lot of risk, that was the way he felt. Well, now"—he began to laugh—"now it's exactly the other way around. Man would sell his soul for a government contract. That's what it's all about, the bluest of the blue chips." He looked at me, smiling. "Everything changes, Brother Tom." I took Gail's arm and moved to go, but he put his hand on my shoulder. "You come back now. Both of you."

I said, "I may come back for the dedication. By the way, you ought to 've told me."

He nodded his big head. "Those idiots in City Hall. I'll talk to them, you should've been notified. It's a hell of a thing, the old man deserved it. What he put into this place, twelve years of his life and not much recognition, I mean nothing material. Tangible. Not much to show for it except this." He meant the agency. "Which has not done badly if I do say so myself." He paused and lit a cigar, then he replaced his hand on my shoulder. "The thing that makes me proudest is that he created the conditions for the boom. It was a hands-off administration, his. The old man believed in progress and no interference, bless his heart. I don't know what the hell he'd think if he saw the shape the country's in now. But he set the climate in Dement, excellent labor relations, strong banks, no problems with the zoning or with the minorities and only the usual problems with the politicians. He would've done fine if he hadn't gone haywire at the end with the Springfield thing. That was a mistake."

Warren grinned, the memory somehow comfortable. "This is a hell of a town. You made a mistake, Brother Tom. You should have stayed. Bill and I, we're going to run this place someday. You could've had a hand in it." He laughed loudly. "We damn near run it now, matter of fact. You ought to trot on over and see it, Lewis School. Dad's name on that school, highly appropriate."

Then: "You know, you look tired. You ought to take a vacation, do the rest of us a favor, hahaha. They ought to declare a vacation in Washington six months of every year, give the country a chance to get on its feet." He rocked back on his heels, expansive now, the cigar protruding from his fist like a gun barrel. "Seriously, you look beat. Any time you want you can have the condo in Lauderdale, just give me some warning. Doesn't cost me a nickel anyhow, it's a write-off. You know what the old man said, 'In a heavy rain, you need a shelter.' Christ," he said. "Christ, I'm sorry to see you out of the business but it's better all around. Hell, it's no secret; you never had the taste for it, Dad knew that. God, Bill and I; ah, the *fun*, Tommy, *the fun of it!*"

Bill had joined us and Warren threw one of his huge arms around Bill's shoulder. The two of them stood grinning, their bodies in motion, arms around each other. Warren shook his head, eyes glittering. Then he cleared his throat. "Now look, you come back here. This is where you're from after all, you come back here and see us now and again, get yourself in touch with the real people. Listen, we want to see you both any time"—he was looking at Gail now, beaming down at her—"I know how difficult it is and how involved you are there, in the East. But you name the time, we want to see you back here in Dement. Certainly you can spare some time for us."

Warren's telephone rang and his young secretary reached across her desk to answer it. "Your people are here, not there. They're here, right? Right?" The secretary motioned to him and he picked up the telephone, cradling it in his hand. I was moving to the door, Gail ahead of me; I thought, What a performance. I was already thinking about the lights of the capital, the long slow descent over the Potomac. I would have to rush, hurry like hell, but I thought I could make the last flight from O'Hare. Warren watched us, his hand cupped over the black mouthpiece. He moved his thighs and smiled. I waved at him and opened the door. "Look," he said. "I'm sorry."

We took off to the south, then banked around and flew over Dement, heading northeast to O'Hare. I was watching the dials; it had been a long time since I'd been in an airplane cockpit. Gail was in the rear, and I took the last empty seat, the copilot's. I asked the pilot about each dial, then turned my attention outside. The triangular city receded to port and I watched it go, moving back of me, the lights feeble now as we gained altitude.

My mind was suddenly crowded with images, the governor's benediction, the seventh-grade teacher of arithmetic, President Warren, Gail's matter of strict fact, Freud's Twenty-third Psalm; all of it crowded my mind, invading my imagination, the images confused. Then I looked back at the city, marveling at the lights abruptly blazing brightly to port. The perimeter of Dement was clearly defined, like the walls of an ancient city or the life of a man. There were no lights at all beyond the perimeter. The cockpit was dark except for the green glow of the instrument panel. The pilot was busy with the instruments. I stretched and craned my neck around, to motion to Gail two seats behind me. But she was turned away, her body slack; apparently she was napping. I stared at her a long moment—I had had the last one once, and might again. She stirred and our eyes met, caressing. Once free, anything was possible. She turned away. Passion, evidence of life. She closed her eyes. I looked down and the lights were still there, bright, burning, conspicuous as stars, and fixed forever.

PART II

1. *Dietz at War*

2. *Journal of a Plague Year*

3. *A Man at the Top of His Trade*

4. *D.*

Dietz at War

Twice or three times a week Dietz wrote his children. They were informal letters that began Dear Girls and ended Much Love from Dad. He liked to describe the country and the hotel in which he lived, and at every opportunity he wrote about the various animals he saw. Around the corner from the hotel was a crippled vendor with a monkey and once a month he'd visit the zoo. The zoo's attractions were a single Bengal tiger and two mangy elephants. The tiger he called Charlie and the two elephants Ike and Mike. In his frequent trips to the countryside he'd see water buffaloes and pigs, and once he'd taken a photograph of a Marine major with an eighteen-foot anaconda wrapped around his neck. Dietz hated snakes but his children didn't. He invented wild and improbable stories about the animals, giving them names and personalities and droll adventures. From time to time he'd give the girls a glimpse into his own life, opening the door a crack and then shutting it again.

73

He thought the letters and his motives for writing them were straightforward, but his former wife did not. On one of Dietz's visits home she told him that the letters were interesting, but not much use to the children. "You're really writing those letters to me," she said.

Dietz was very serious about the letters; in three years in the war zone he missed a week just once. He wrote the letters early in the morning, before he began the day's work. When he expected to be out of touch for any length of time he'd leave several letters with the concierge of the hotel, with instructions to mail one every three days. It was important to him to be part of the lives of his children, and he considered the letters as valuable and necessary substitutes for personal visits. The letters were as long as they needed to be, and were posted with exotic stamps.

However, he was careful never to disclose too much. Because he lived in a war zone he felt entitled to keep his personal life to himself. He did not want to alarm or upset the children, nor did he want to leave the impression he was enjoying himself. He thought if he phrased the letters with care the girls would understand his obligations to himself and to his work. Dietz never had the slightest feeling of heroism, still less of advancing any national interest. He was a newspaper correspondent and believed in journalism. He believed in his value as an expert witness whose testimony might one day prove valuable. The work was demanding and not to everyone's taste, but Dietz found it congenial. Because the war zone was dangerous he felt he had the right to make his own rules, and that meant the right to withhold certain information from his children and the others.

There were several love affairs, and many friends both male and female. During the worst part of the war scarcely a week went by without someone he knew, or knew of, being wounded or killed. There was one terrible week when five correspondents were killed and a number of others wounded, but Dietz did not mention this to the children except in an oblique way. In a letter home he told a long and compli-

cated animal story and assigned the names of the dead to various enchanting animals. Dietz felt in that way he commemorated his colleagues.

He worked eighteen-hour days and considered himself at the top
of his craft. Everyone he knew had difficult personal problems that
obliged them to sail close to the wind, as his friend Puller expressed it.
Puller described the war zone as a neurotics' retreat no less than the
Elizabeth Arden beauty farm or the Esalen Institute. While recognizing
the truth of what Puller said, Dietz did not apply it to his own life. The
various personal problems, serious as they might appear to outsiders,
were not allowed to interfere with the job he was paid to do.

Therefore, the letters home were not factual but invented. Dietz
did not completely understand this until years later, when he chanced
upon the correspondence and reread it. Dietz kept carbons of everything
he wrote.

Odd—there was not a line in any of the letters about the good times
he'd had. It was awkward to talk of good times because people put you
down as a war lover, a man who drew pleasure from the suffering of
others. And from *this* war, no less. Borrowing a concept from older
writers who had covered earlier wars, Dietz told himself that a sense of
carelessness and adventure was necessary in order to remain sane. In
order not to become permanently depressed. He explained this idea one
night to an experienced woman who had witnessed a number of European wars and she laughed in his face, not unkindly. The other wars were
sane, she said. This war was insane.

"And?"

"Draw your own conclusions."

Still, in his letters home, there was not a word about casual things
—pleasant walks through the damp scented air in the deserted parks
early in the morning. Nothing about late-night swims in the pool at the
old country club, or afternoons at the run-down racetrack. Nothing
about the long evenings playing bridge, or the occasional sprees at

restaurants in the Chinese quarter. There was nothing at all about the constant noisy laughter as the correspondents drifted down the boulevard to a café where there were drinks and hot roasted peanuts in shallow dishes. There were no descriptions or explanations of the many wonderful friendships he'd made.

While there was nothing at all in the letters about the good times, there was nothing about the bad times either.

Having decided to cut himself off from America, Dietz felt it was important and necessary to take an aggressively neutral stance in his attitude toward the war. He felt that the one could only be justified in terms of the other—for he had *fled* the United States, no question about that. This belief was reflected both in the letters and in the articles he wrote. His heaviest gun was irony. Dietz acquired an uncommon ability to turn sentences in such a way that left his readers empty and puzzled and, when he was writing at the top of his form, depressed. The facts he selected implied foreboding, and his descriptions suggested darkness and disease. This was done subtly. He wheeled his irony into position at the end of every story, and gave his readers a salvo. Standing outside events, even-handed Dietz believed he was uniquely equipped to describe an enterprise that was plainly misconceived: deformed, doomed. He never wrote of anything as crude and obvious as wounded children or wrecked churches. Instead, he devoted a series of articles to the remarkable military hospitals and their talented surgeons, who saved lives and left men vegetables or worse. He became something of a social historian, describing the furious whims and customs of those involved in the war. Dietz developed a theory that there was a still center in the middle of the war, a safe location without vibrations of any kind, and if he could occupy that center he could present the war from a disinterested position. A moral fortress. It would be the more precise and persuasive for being factually impartial, because it was evident to him that the public was skeptical of anything that hinted at the lurid or the grotesque. Dietz worked at trimming adjectives from his prose, and was careful to spell everything out with near-mathematical precision.

He wanted to describe the war with the delicacy and restraint of Henry James setting forth the details of a love affair.

His life enlarged and grew in harmony with the war. He was rooted, comfortable and at ease, feeling himself outside the war and inside it at the same time. Dietz refused to learn the history of the country or its language or the origins of the struggle, in the belief that the war was necessarily a sentient experience. He brought emotion to his portraiture, but the emotions were solidly based on fact.

He was scrupulous. Aircraft, artillery, small arms, battalions, battlefields—all of them were precisely identified by name, number, or location. Dietz's room at the hotel was covered with American military maps, and he'd obtained weapons manuals from a friendly colonel at American military headquarters. Readers understood immediately where they were and what was happening, who was doing the fighting, and with what weaponry, and the name and age of the dead and wounded. These facts, so precise and unassailable, gave Dietz's journalism the stamp of authenticity and therefore of authority. Dietz believed that facts described the truth in the same way that shapes and colors describe a landscape, and in that way journalism resembled art.

One April afternoon he was almost killed.

They'd encouraged him to accompany a long-range patrol. They did not conceal its danger: this was a reconnaissance patrol that would establish beyond any doubt the existence of sanctuaries in the supposedly neutral country to the west. They were frank to say that public knowledge of these sanctuaries would be . . . helpful. Dietz was free to write what he pleased, and of course it was entirely possible that there would be no sanctuaries. But they trusted Dietz to write what he saw.

Dietz was eager, listening to them explain the mission. This was not a patrol that would engage the enemy. It was purely reconnaissance for the purpose of intelligence gathering. But they did not lie to him about the danger. There was at least an even chance that the patrol would be discovered in some way, and that would mean serious trouble. They would be deep in enemy territory. However, the commander would be the best reconnaissance man in the zone and his team would be hand-picked. It would be an all-volunteer force. A helicopter squadron would monitor their progress and be prepared for immediate action. The mission had the highest priority and Dietz was free to go along without restraint. It was appealing, the story was appealing on a number of levels; Dietz put danger out of his mind.

On the second day the patrol was ambushed and nearly annihilated. The commander and his number two were killed, and Dietz and half a dozen others were wounded. They owed their lives to the quick reaction time of the helicopter force, though for an hour they were obliged to defend themselves without aid of any kind. Of course they found no sanctuaries or anything else of value, and in that sense the mission was a failure.

Dietz was five days in a field hospital, half-delirious and very weak from loss of blood. They watched him around the clock. As soon as they were able, the authorities moved him to a small private clinic in the capital. Having urged him to undertake the mission, they now felt responsible. They'd make certain he had the best medical attention available in the zone.

In ten days the danger was past, though the effects lingered. Dietz was euphoric.

His friend Puller, looking at him lying in bed, remarked, "You look like hell."

"Feel fine," Dietz said.

"White as a sheet," Puller said.

"Lost all my blood," Dietz said.

"You need a drink. Can you have a drink?"

Dietz laughed and extended his hand, and Puller poured him a gin and tonic.

"Actually you look okay."

The nurse was working on his arm, cutting the steel sutures that bound his wounds. "It's a load off my mind," Dietz said.

"How's that?"

"This can only happen to you once. The odds. I've used up my ticket."

Puller looked at the nurse and asked her in French how Dietz was.

The nurse said, Fine. Recovery was rapid.

How long would Dietz remain in the hospital?

Perhaps a week, the nurse said. But he would have to remain quiet when he got out. He'd sustained shock and was more disoriented than he realized. If Monsieur Dietz were wise, he'd take a long holiday.

Puller observed that his friend seemed in very good spirits.

The nurse nodded, Indeed. A model patient, always cheerful.

Puller turned back to Dietz. "I talked with your office on the telephone today." He smiled. "They wanted to know when to expect the story."

"I'm writing it in my head," Dietz said.

"Well, they said not to worry. They're giving you a month's leave, you can have it whenever you want it. They'd like you to return to the States for a couple of weeks. But you can do what you want."

Dietz winced as the nurse washed and dried the large wound on his forearm. "Ask her how long I'll be in here."

"You really don't know any French at all?"

"Only the basics," Dietz said.

Puller smiled; Dietz made no concessions. He was the same wherever he was, the Middle East, Latin America. He didn't know Arabic or Spanish either. He was like a camera, his settings operated in any environment. "She says you'll be out in a week but you'll have to take it easy."

Dietz pointed to a pile of mail on the bureau. There was a foot-high stack of letters and telegrams. "Did you pick up any mail today?"

"None for you," Puller said.

Dietz looked puzzled. "Nothing at all?"

"You're a greedy bastard. Christ, you've heard from everybody but the Secretary of Defense."

"I love to read expressions of sympathy," Dietz said.

"When are you going to write the story?"

"Well, I told you. I am writing it. In my head."

"I mean for the newspaper."

"I have to write it for the kids first."

"Oh, sure," Puller said.

"I have to get the characters straight. These stories are damned complicated, and the kids count on them."

"Right."

". . . got to get the plot worked out."

"Do you want your portable?"

"No, I'm writing it in my head, memorizing it. I'll memorize it and write it up in longhand. But it's taking a hell of a long time, I'm only up to the first night." He smiled benignly. "Bivouac."

Puller put two ice cubes and a finger of gin in Dietz's drink, watching the nurse frown and turn away. He told Dietz that he had to leave but would look in at dinnertime, perhaps bring a few friends. He moved to go, then looked back at the bed. "What did you mean a moment ago, that you've used up your ticket? What does that mean?"

"I'm invulnerable. This can only happen to you once. The odds are all in my favor. I've done everything now, I'm clean. They've got nothing on me."

"I'd like to know the name of that odds-maker. That bastard is practicing without a license."

Dietz laughed. "It's true!"

"And who hasn't got anything on you?"

"They don't. None of them do." Dietz said, "I've paid my dues." That was a private joke and they both laughed. "I'm in fat city."

"Jesus Christ," Puller muttered. "I suppose you are, as long as you're here."

Dietz drained his glass and grinned. "When you come back tonight, bring me some stationery. The kids are probably worried, they haven't heard from me in two weeks. Probably don't know where the hell I am."

Puller nodded, Sure. Then: "Well, they know you got hit."

"No reason for them to."

"But—"

"Listen. It's a long story, so bring plenty of stationery."

"Honest to God, you look in damn good shape," Puller said.

"Feel fine," said Dietz.

In the end Dietz wrote a story for the children and the newspaper, and they were entirely different stories. The story for the children was witty, crammed with incident and populated with strange animal characters in a mythical setting. He set one character against the others, though all of them were friends. The story began darkly but ended sweetly, it was very exciting and covered twelve sheets of paper. In the act of writing it, Dietz discarded most of the myths and composed a lovable story about animals. The article for the newspaper was deft and straightforward. He wrote the article in one draft from memory and did not consult his notebook at all. Reading it over, he was alarmed to find he'd neglected his facts, save the central incident and one or two names. To his surprise and confusion it was a cruel but cheerful story, and somehow uplifting despite its savage details. He kept himself out of it and most readers did not understand until the final sentences that it was an eyewitness account. But the editors liked it and put it on page one with a box and a picture of Dietz. The picture caption read: "Dietz at War."

He cabled the story, then did a strange thing. He wrote the editor of the newspaper and told him to inform his ex-wife when the article would be published. The editor was to tell the ex-wife to keep the newspaper out of the house that day. Under no circumstances were the children to see the article Dietz had written about himself.

Dietz went from success to success. He matured with the war, developing a singular style of journalism in order to arrive at the still center of the violence. In the years following the murderous afternoon in April he devoted himself entirely to journalism and to his letters home. He removed himself from the life of the capital and ventured ever farther afield for his stories. He'd spend two weeks among the mountain people, then a week investigating the political structure of an obscure coastal province. His dispatches contained detailed descriptions of the flora and fauna of the country, its landscapes and population. There were many places where the war was not present and he was careful to visit those as well. Often Dietz's stories contained no more than two or three facts—the dateline, the subject, the subject's age. No more, often less.

But his sense of irony, his understanding of awful paradox, was exquisite. He saw the war in delicate balance and reported it as he would report the life and atmosphere of an asylum, or zoo. He adopted various points of view in his reportage, convinced that each moment possessed its own life; he often impersonated a traveler from abroad. Energetic and restless in his inquiries, he occasionally published fictitious information. These were the devices he used to move the emotions of his readers. As the dead piled on dead his images became blacker and more melancholy, though he fought for balance. He'd bring himself back into equilibrium by writing a long letter to his children. Every month he spent at least a fortnight with troops on the line, though he always refused to carry a weapon.

During one of the periodic cease-fires (they came as interregnums, pauses between seizures), Dietz's old friend Puller returned from the United States. Puller'd done a year's time in the zone and departed without hesitation. That was two years ago, and now Puller was back for a visit. They spent a long and sour night drinking in Dietz's hotel room.

Puller demanded, "Why are you still here? No one cares anymore, what are you doing here?"

"I live here. It's my home."

"It's a forgotten front, I'll tell you that."

"Not by me."

"No one gives a damn anymore."

"Well, I do."

"Odds in your favor, is that it?"

"Well, I'm here. In one piece. Healthy. Sound."

"You ought to quit it," Puller said. "There's a limit—"

"It's a rich vein," Dietz said. "Hardly touched."

"A vein of pure crap."

"The rest of you, it's all right. You can watch it from the United States. The point is, you can't *know* this place until you've lived here. You have to *live* here, in it."

Puller looked at him. "It's a place like any other. One more place to get stale in."

"You think I'm stale?"

"The stuff you're writing, a lot of it doesn't make any sense."

"Are you reading it?"

"Well, no. I don't read it much anymore."

Dietz smiled. His expression was one of satisfaction. "Well, it's strange. Perhaps true." He smiled warmly, and poured fresh drinks for them both. "You know, because of the cease-fire there's been no dead this week. No killed or wounded. No casualty lists." He shrugged, amused, amazed. The casualty lists had been part of his life for so long that he could not imagine their absence. They and the war were what he lived with. He had not come to terms with parting from either of them, the dead or the war. America seemed to him remote, at an infinite remove; the back of beyond. "None," he said.

"You think you're *part* of this war. You think you can't leave it. You think that if you go away, the war will disappear."

"No man is indispensable." Dietz grinned.

"Paying your dues. You're *paid up!*" Puller glanced around the familiar room, it hadn't changed in two years. The transistor radio, the bottles on the sideboard, the photograph over the typewriter—Dietz in fatigues, fording a nameless river in the jungle. Puller had taken the picture, catching Dietz's winning smile as the water washed over his chest. Dietz had hung the picture—why? Perhaps it reminded him of hardship. Whenever he looked up from the typewriter he saw himself in fatigues, fording some nameless river, smiling.

"Yes, I am," Dietz agreed.

"Then why—"

Dietz roared, "My God, Puller—how can that compare to *this?*"

Puller left shortly after midnight (they were both drunk, and less friendly than at the beginning), and Dietz prepared another drink and set about securing himself for the night. A hotel room was a world away, a haven in its safety and invisibility; its neutrality. No man's land. Drink in hand, he set the latch and the chain and the bolt, and tucked the desk chair under the doorknob. He checked the tape that crisscrossed the windows that looked out onto the main square of the capital; on advice of army friends, he'd taped the windows to prevent flying glass in the event of an explosion. He locked the windows and carefully removed the pictures from the walls and stacked them under the bed, where they'd be safe. The bottles of gin and whiskey were placed in the closet, next to the carbine and the filled canteens. There was a full clip of ammunition taped to the stock of the carbine; he inspected that to verify that it was clean, and that the breech was oiled and the barrel spotless. His steel pot and knapsack were in their places, on the shelf in the clothes closet. He drew the blinds and covered his typewriter and put the table lamp on the floor next to his desk.

Dietz took a long pull on his drink and looked around the room, satisfied. He undressed slowly, taking small sips every few seconds. He listened for any disturbance in the street but heard nothing. The sentry was still in the square—how did they expect one man to fend off an attack, if it came? The sentry was leaning against a lamppost like some dapper soak in a Peter Arno cartoon; it was useless, he was probably asleep. He was either asleep or working for the other side. The most dangerous time was between midnight and 3 A.M., he'd learned that much from the military authorities. It was during the early-morning hours that the enemy struck without warning, moving anonymously from the shadows, planting satchel charges and mines. A month earlier there'd been a scare in the hotel and half a dozen downtown restaurants were now off limits to American personnel. His drink empty, Dietz flicked on an overhead light and the two lamps next to his bed. The desk lamp on the floor was already burning, as were the lights in the bathroom. He stripped and lay naked on the sheets, listening to the hum of the air-conditioner. Then he reached for his pen, and the box of stationery.

Dietz never wearied of writing to his children. Over the years the letters grew prolix, four and five letters a week, some of them five and six hundred words long. Dear Girls, Much Love from Dad. It didn't bother him that his children didn't reply for months at a time, and it did not occur to him at all that one of them was too young to write anything. His former wife, suddenly sympathetic, kept him informed of their progress. He had not been to America in more than three years; his vacations were limited to long weekends at a secure seaside resort. He felt it would be a tragedy to be out of the country the day it "blew," so he kept himself in constant readiness. He invented wonderful stories about the animals in the zoo, and his letters home were entirely concerned with the Bengal tiger, the two elephants, the zebra, the monkey, the antelope, the water buffalo, the snake, and the civet cat. These animals were assigned personalities that corresponded to the men who managed the war.

Dietz stayed on in the zone, assembling ever more powerful ironies with which to ravage the consciences of his readers. After five years the management of the newspaper insisted that he come home for good. When he refused, the publisher of the paper sent him a brief note informing him that he would either come home or consider himself fired. Dietz scanned the note and decided there were loopholes, they would not dare to fire him. He'd plead for time, and if necessary take leave and file on a free-lance basis. He knew that in the last analysis they would not fire him; they never fired anybody.

Dietz's critics insisted that he was out of touch with the realities of the war. It was no longer a war but a depredation. The realities had changed but Dietz had not. He was rarely seen at the various important news briefings, preferring instead to investigate the mood of the provinces. In the provinces he found life and therefore hope and from time to time a strange sweetness infused his copy. He had long since given up his love affairs and was an infrequent visitor to the downtown cafés. It was true that his ironic turn of mind no longer puzzled or depressed his readers, as it was true his children found his letters home tedious. However, his readers still thought him authoritative and his children assured him they loved him. He was a majestic figure inside his moral fortress, healthy, astute, and entirely free of bias. In that way the war never lost its savor, and Dietz was free of facts forever.

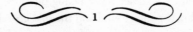

Journal of a Plague Year

1

In the afternoon the shooting stopped and the dead were lying under the rubber trees on canvas stretchers. There were eight dead and an aid tent nearby with a dozen wounded. It was hot and very still. The grove of rubber trees was situated on a flat plain, inland from the sea; the plain was littered with military machinery. Naval gunfire was still falling, and they could hear the explosions a mile or two away. Soldiers were sprawled under the trees, smoking dope and drinking beer and talking quietly. Someone had a radio turned to AFRTS, and the soldiers' heads nodded to the beat. They paid no attention to the dead, who were covered with green rubber ponchos; the dead blended into the vegetation, and after a while they were scarcely noticeable at all. They might have been men sleeping, unless you looked closely at their hands, which were rigid and gray.

She noticed that their boots looked new, hardly worn at all; two of the rifles had not been fired; they had full clips and were still on safety. She wrote these details in her notebook. She had no desire to see the faces, but she wondered if the dead had head wounds, and whether the wounds were gunshot or shrapnel. The colonel had told her they had run into snipers, and the wounded men in the tent confirmed that. The colonel said he had never seen such accurate sniper fire, and his lead element had lost a dozen dead and wounded in the first few minutes. They had been moving through the rubber trees on line, and had taken all their casualties in the first half hour. Those included the company commander and his RTO. It took a while for the company to regroup and understand where the fire was coming from. Officially, the report read that they had bumped an enemy battalion. But hell, the colonel said, it could have been just a few enemy; five or six snipers, who'd been very cool and deliberate about their business. Sniping, he said; that was a tactic that one way or another dated back to the Peloponnesian Wars, Athens and Sparta. There was nothing new or different about sniping.

She stood a little distance away taking pictures, framing the shot to catch the dead in the foreground and the soldiers relaxing in the rear. She shot a dozen pictures in different focuses, to make the ironic point. There were a number of ways to get various effects: blur the foreground and sharp-focus the rear, or vice versa. Or use the depth of field to pull the entire picture in sharp. She practiced with different settings, regulating the light and shade, although everything would depend on the darkroom and how it was handled there. Not that it made any difference; they seldom printed her pictures.

Someone handed her a can of beer and she sat down, cradling the camera. The dead were at eye level now, and she took the camera and shot the rest of the film, shooting with the boots in the foreground. It was a disgusting and witless business, but she was there for a purpose, and she thought she ought to get all she could. Just then she knew that someone was looking at her, and the vibrations were not friendly. Without glancing up she put the camera away, stuffing it hard into her rucksack and staring straight ahead. After a moment or two she shifted her eyes, and saw a soldier staring at her. The soldier's face was hard with hatred. After a minute, he looked away. Then she got up and walked away to find the landing zone, and a helicopter that would take her back to Division.

That night they were all drinking in the third-floor suite and quite early she left with another journalist to have a nightcap and then go to bed. They had one or two drinks; the journalist wanted to talk about his love affair with an airline stewardess. He was wondering if he should ask his office to extend his tour. His paper sent their correspondents on six-month tours; the assignment was passed around the office like a penalty.

"See, she's based out of Hong Kong and I could work at least three more visits there if I'd apply for an extension. Christ, I'm really in love with her. Fallen for her, you know?"

"I'd reapply, then." She was thinking about her story, the fight that afternoon. She could write the story around the interviews with the wounded and the colonel, folding in some description of the grove of rubber trees and the dead. She could write it from the point of view of the enemy.

"I hate this goddamned town, and the war that goes with it. This crummy hotel and the money-grubbing people." He took a long swallow of his drink, staring at her over the edge of the glass.

What did you say to that? It was better in the field?

"She's something, look at this." He handed over a picture of a very blond girl in a bikini. "This was taken on one of the beaches in Hong Kong. She's nice, no? She's a swinger, that's really what she likes to do in life. It was a hell of a lot of fun in Hong Kong. We went shopping. I got a Nikon and some threads. Three fittings in three days." He paused, smiling. "You ought to find a man."

"Is one lost?"

"Something permanent for a little while."

They sat quietly, drinking the last of a bottle of scotch. It was near midnight; she thought she ought to be in bed. She wondered whether to write the story that night or in the morning. She thought it was better to write it fresh, with no complications. The other started to talk about his stewardess again, how she had changed his life. He said she was uninhibited, that was the best part about her. The voodoo princess from BOAC. He was very relaxed and happy, sitting back in the big chair. All the rooms of the hotel were similar, same beds, same furniture. A stereo set in the corner, freshly laundered fatigues hanging on a hook near the door; military gear, knapsacks and canteens. She felt pleasantly tired; it had been a strain making three airplane connections from the field. They finished the last of their drinks and she got up to go.

"She's a hell of a girl."

"Al, you're the envy of your friends."

"Why don't you stay?"

She laughed and stepped into the silent hall and walked down to the elevator. She was excited at the thought of writing the story in the morning, two pots of coffee in the room. She'd take three, four hours writing the story, then have a long and languid lunch. No, not the elevator; there was a better idea. She walked down two floors and knocked on another door, after listening quietly for a moment and hearing music from within. The door opened a notch.

"It's me," she said.

"Back from the wars."

She leaned against the doorjamb, and smiled.

"It's late," he said.

"Ten minutes of talk," she said. "Then I'll go."

The door opened wider and she walked in. He climbed back into bed. She was carrying two note pads, and she put those on the night table. Then she stretched out on the bed and kissed his elbow. He smiled and touched her cheek. He was reading one of Céline's books, the book open and lying on his chest.

She was suddenly very sleepy. "I don't know how you can read novels of that kind, here, in this place. The place is crazy enough without compounding it. I think one's reading ought to be very highly structured. Sears catalogs. The Book of Genesis. Shakespeare's sonnets. Captured enemy documents. Céline will drive you crazy. Everything that's in Céline is present here as well. There are a number of very important concepts here that Céline has not begun to touch."

"Invincible ignorance," he said.

She yawned, very sleepy now.

"You would be better informed if you read Céline."

"Crazier," she mumbled.

"Did you get a good story today?"

"Unh."

"Make notes? Did you get to the bones of the myth? Did you count the dead? Did the dead count you? How many puzzled expressions today? Any fanciful explanations?"

"Thought about you," she said. Her eyes were closed; she could feel his palm. She was almost asleep. He was speaking very softly to her, touching her head and her neck. She moved closer to him, dreaming about him. She dreamed they were in bed together, making love. She dreamed he loved her, they loved each other. She was dreaming before she was asleep.

When she woke in the morning he was gone.

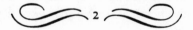

In the fall she went home on leave, back to Washington. She found Washington nervous and agitated, though the weather was gorgeous. It was a poisonous atmosphere, and she endured three Washington dinner parties where she was lectured on the war. They had all the textbook answers, orders of battle, force levels, kill ratios, free fire zones, A and B levels of pacification, endurance estimates, morale factors—all of them classified. Washington was harsh and metallic, edges everywhere.

She received three cables from him. She stayed with friends and watched television programs in the evening, news reports from the war zone. It was peculiar, seeing her friends on television, watching them doing their stand-ups with gunfire in the background. Seeing the streets of the city, more familiar to her now than any American city, she bored her friends with travelogues. Her paper obliged her to deliver lectures, and she found she could not talk persuasively about what she had seen. She had no powers of recall. She could write about it, but she could not talk about it; the emotion was something within. The lectures were a failure except for one television appearance when she spoke from notes. Reading the notes afterward, she decided that what she'd said were lies. She related these episodes to him in a long letter that took her most of a morning to write; it was difficult to connect their lives.

But in Washington they thought it was fantastic, what she was doing. Fan*tas*tic. They thought she made a difference, made them uncomfortable in the Department of Defense. The trouble with Washington, they said, was that it was too comfortable. She reached them with her war stories, she was way down deep.

"Whatever they're paying you, it's not enough."

"It's enough," she said.

"No, really. It's fantastic. Are you going to stay for long? Six months more? A year? You ought to think about a return to America, and reporting from Capitol Hill. They're crying for women now. You could write your own ticket. Do such a good job. I don't know how you stand it, where you are."

"Invincible ignorance," she said.

"Oh, we know how it is. You don't have to play that role with us. We know how it must be, or perhaps we don't. Perhaps we can't conceive. But you're well read."

She was confused, two or three of them were talking at once. For a lunatic moment she felt like one of those Japanese soldiers who are found on Guam or Saipan or somewhere, holding out twenty-six years after the surrender. It put her off to be told that the stories were being read, although, of course, she knew that; but it was better knowing it at a distance. It seemed to her that people were looking over her shoulder. She took a drink from a passing waiter and backed away.

"God," one of them breathed. They were being very solicitous, kind in their way. But it was an invasion, and what was she supposed to say?

"If you're telling the truth in your stories, then it must be the most dreadful place. Crazy. I mean, crazed. Don't you hate the war? Though it's exciting, of course. It's a hell, it must be sixth or seventh circle. No kidding now, just how bad is it? On the other hand, you must be making a bundle."

"I'm the happiest I've been," she said.

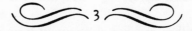

She made her way west, cabling him from San Francisco. She gave him her flight number and time of arrival. She was enthusiastic, flying into the city; she'd decided that if she was so valuable and fantastic, then she could fly first class. She was going to stop in Tokyo, but decided against that. She would come in straight as a die from southern California, reading books and listening to tapes. A bottle of wine, no sleep, sunrise over the Pacific. There was plenty of time for thought, five miles above the Pacific Ocean. She was sorry now that she'd left the war. Washington had given her nothing; home leave was a misnomer. She had to be arch about it, and tell them that she did not relate to the environment. Everything in Washington was pale by comparison; there was nothing to be seen with the eyes. It was antiseptic. Washington was insincere, it had no structure, its life was loose and at odds. He'd asked her to buy some books for him in America, and she had those in her carry bag. It was a gaudy assortment: Robbe-Grillet, Bernard Fall's latest book, *Bleak*

House, Black Mischief, A Sentimental Education, the short novels of Henry James. She wondered how Henry James would relate to the environment, how Henry James would handle the five o'clock briefing. Follow that through: it was a turn of the screw removed from the Home Counties and Pall Mall. It was a pleasure buying the books, and having them with her.

In a rumpled dress, swinging the carry bag, she alighted from the airplane in heat of a hundred degrees. She stood to one side at the base of the ramp, searching for him in the crowd. The other passengers swept past her, construction foremen, diplomats, army officers, people who in one way or another were involved in the war. She didn't see him on the tarmac; strange, because he said he'd be there. She walked toward the waiting room, sad, searching with her eyes. She was anxious to see him, and slightly panicked now; she'd thought there was something formidable and intimate about his meeting the airplane. The place was entirely familiar to her.

She saw him then, standing alone against the wall of the waiting room, staring straight ahead, puzzled. He looked at her, then past her. His eyes floated past, his hands were in his pockets. She walked up to him, smiling—and when he saw her he gave a little start, and grinned shyly. He shook his head, as if he'd awakened from a nap. She kissed him, unaware that anything was wrong.

"I've got your books."

"Oh, good."

"They're in the carry bag, all of them. I couldn't get one of them in French. All they had was the English."

"I don't mind."

"But the rest of them are here. James and the others." She opened the carry bag so he could see the books.

"Well, how was it? Did you like it? I'm sorry about the cables, but I was worried when I didn't hear."

"I didn't like it at all. If it's news to you, *they're* the ones behind bars, in straitjackets. I'm glad to be back. To be here with you."

The passengers were moving past them; there was a long line at customs. He motioned to the bar in the waiting room. They were in no hurry, and it was useless to try to accelerate the customs process. Customs proceeded at a deliberate pace.

"I've got a car outside. Let's have a drink, then go through the line."

"It's *so* long, I'll get in line now."

"It's an hour either way."

"Maybe there'll be someone that we know. You wait. I'll go through now."

He saw small beads of perspiration on her forehead and cheeks. She hated the heat; it affected her badly. He dried her forehead with the back of his hand, and kissed her again. She smiled and gripped his arm. He kissed her again, more gently, then drew away. She looked weary, tired, and drawn.

"Are you all right?"

She smiled brightly and nodded. The heat.

"No, seriously."

"I'm on pins and needles," she said, still smiling.

"Let's get a drink."

"No, I'll go through the line. I'll be very quick."

He shrugged. "Sure. When will the war end?"

They didn't talk much in the car, and later, in the hotel, they circled each other, wary. They made love very roughly. He was not with her, and she knew then that something was very wrong. She pressed him for explanations, but it was useless. He said it was impossible to explain correctly, so he would not explain at all. He looked at her strangely, as if he'd expected someone else; usually so cheerful, he did not smile at all. The next day he moved out of their hotel room to an apartment near the cathedral. He said that life was confusing, and she wished him good luck on that. She had her work, but she was sorry just the same. He was as much a part of her life as the work. But she was stoic about it, there being no real alternative; she would stay busy, and would not lack company. Mystified, she let him be, to work out whatever it was.

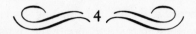

Circumstances drew them together again. Much later, when he'd tried everything to get her back, and had been successful in a temporary way, he told her about the morning at the airport, and what had happened later. She didn't want to hear about it particularly, but he told her anyway. He said he could describe it, but not explain it; the emotions were complicated. He said he hadn't recognized her. "You were some-one else altogether. I didn't recognize you until you were five feet away, looking me in the face. I saw you standing at the bottom of the ramp, but I didn't know . . . who you were. Three weeks was a millennium. You were a stranger. I didn't know what to expect. Until we were face to face, and I saw you smiling at me, I didn't connect. I knew that it had to be you, because you were looking at me in a special way, and when you spoke I recognized your voice. You looked like you ought to look, and then you kissed me. But your face was unfamiliar. Were you differ-ent in some way? I thought so, but I didn't understand it. You were a stranger, so later when we were together it was like being with a stranger. And to have that, after everything that had happened before. You: a woman casually picked out of a crowd at an airport, a woman in a slept-in dress and an old carry bag. A beautiful woman bringing books, neither young nor old. I could've died. In a week or two, I knew you again, but it was a different acquaintance. I remembered all the things we'd done together. But that morning at the airport, the surface escaped me."

She understood him. To her sorrow she knew exactly what he meant. "This place has no memory," she said. "If anything leaves, it's forgotten, and if it returns, it has to begin again. No memory, no loyalties."

"No moving parts," he said.

She shook her head and sighed. "It was pretty bad in the hotel room."

"I'm sorry about it," he said.

"I know."

"I didn't understand."

She gave him a rueful little smile. "How could you?" she asked.

They lived together on tiptoe, quietly and conservatively, stepping lightly, under strain. They reported to each other as they reported the war, at a distance. They became oddly domesticated, as toward the end of her tour she began to avoid the battlefield. She avoided small units, and except for one week with the Navy never left the city for more than two days at a time. She knew what to expect in the field; there was nothing more to say about the dead. There was neither virtue, nor innocence, nor anything else except paradox; even irony, her most reliable weapon, was worn out. She took her evidence, the scenes and the dialogue, from radio operators in colonels' tents. Interviews in hospital wards. After-action reports. Ex post facto accounts. Briefings. She knew all the colonels now, and two or three of them were at pains to alert her when a major operation was under way. She convinced herself that the war had moved into a political phase, and that the battlefield story was less important than the political one. Coincidentally, this happened to be true. But she was still wonderful at what she did, supplying immediacy and drama to the episodes of the war. That did not change, though everything else did.

At length he left for America, and they maintained a sporadic correspondence. She reported on activities in the provinces, he on the atmosphere in Washington. These were detailed, factual letters, suitable for a collection. She would write the letters as carefully as she wrote her newspaper articles, and assumed he did likewise. But nothing was the same after the afternoon in the airport. She didn't know whose fault it was, or if it was anyone's fault; but there were no more dreams in any case. She remembered his words often, and they were troubling. She had always thought of herself as a stranger—and what if that were true after all? Where did that leave her?

3

A Man at the Top of His Trade

He told them to hold all calls, except any that might come from her. There was no reason for her to call, but that was no guarantee that she wouldn't. She often called. Once several weeks ago she'd called and insisted on being put through, and there'd been an awkward five minutes while he muttered into the telephone and the others sat silently looking at their fingernails or otherwise pretending that they weren't listening. Of course, they couldn't hear what he was saying; he normally spoke into the phone in a guttural, a tone so soft that it couldn't be heard more than a foot away. That night when he asked her about it she'd laughed and said her only demand on him was instant access. When she was blue and wanted to talk, he'd have to listen. That was his half of the bargain.

His colleagues were due now, five of them. He'd had the chairs arranged just so, in a semicircle in front of his desk. Ashtrays within easy reach. Pads and pencils on the chairs. There was a conference room across the hall, but Stone didn't like it. The conference room was formal, and this discussion did not need formality. At exactly ten-thirty they had a radio hookup with Browne.

Stone lit a cigarette, thinking about Browne. He'd be preparing his notes now in the tank in the basement of the embassy, the lead-lined color-coordinated "module" sunk like a squash court below the foundations of the building. It was a completely secure room; Stone had helped with the design. Data banks lined one wall; the technology was phenomenal: computers scrambled the voice at one end and unscrambled it at the other, a fresh matrix for each transmission. That had been the true breakthrough. The number of available matrices was virtually infinite, encoding and decoding accomplished in two and a half seconds. Stone had made a hundred transmissions from that same office, before they'd made him an inside man. In his mind's eye he saw Browne sitting in the swivel chair, checking the control panel. He smiled; thirty minutes in the tank could seem a brief life.

Browne felt the same way. Their careers and personalities were similar in many ways; perhaps there was a pattern to their trade. They worked well together, always had; it was on Stone's strong recommendation that Browne had succeeded him as chief of station in C———. And he'd been excellent, though the station had declined in importance. However, that was no fault of Browne's; it was a reflection of changing times and attitudes and priorities. Now Browne was out too; this was his last operation. He could not see Browne as an inside man any more than he had seen himself as an inside man, two years ago. But Browne would adapt. He would be very good as an inside man, though he worried about the girl, Chris. When Browne left C———, Chris would go with him. Well, he was a professional. Stone and Browne were both professionals.

The buzzer sounded, and Stone picked up the telephone. The five of them were in the outer office, waiting.

They would have thirty minutes of discussion before the transmission. The split was two to two, with Otto on the fence as usual. All of them understood that the decision was Stone's, but if the disagreement was profound, they'd be obliged to file a dissent. They knew that Stone would want to avoid that. Stone did not like what he called "pieces of paper" circulating around the building. Stone had a passion for unanimity.

Stone opened the discussion. "The position is this. Browne has to have a definite go or no-go by eleven A.M. It's short notice, but it can't be helped. Everything in the way of transport is laid on. If the decision is go, Browne meets his man"—Stone looked over the tops of his eyeglasses, smiling—"under the clock at the Biltmore . . ." This was the customary euphemism; there was no need for these men to know where the meeting was taking place; that was an operational detail strictly under Stone's control. ". . . at noon. Browne and his man get in the car. There's a second car and a third car. Classic procedure, and we anticipate no difficulties. We've got an airplane that will have him in Brussels in three hours and at Andrews by tomorrow morning." He looked at his watch. "Comment?"

"You have no doubts about his authenticity?"

"Browne is completely confident," Stone said.

Otto asked, "And you?"

"I have doubts about everything. I always have doubts; that's one reason I'm here. But I've satisfied myself that he's genuine."

"What makes Brownie so sure?"

Stone hesitated a moment before replying. "Instinct."

"The approach came out of the blue, is that right?"

Stone nodded. "Over the transom."

"A week ago?"

"No, three days. And he wanted to do it now. Right now."

Jason McAlvin looked at Otto, then at Stone. "The procedure seems sound, and I agree that he's probably genuine. In the past we've gone on a lot less. But I think the main question is, What does he have? What can he give us? And the answer to that is, military intelligence. Right?" McAlvin looked at the men grouped around the desk. "Well, we're quite up to date on that. I have a sufficiency of information. I believe that what we'll get from this man is corroboration. Useful but not decisive. I don't think he'll be able to give us much that is new. Perhaps a scrap here and there. But hell's bells, when you think of the effort that's going to go into it. *His* care and feeding for the next year, maybe two years. That's a lot of coin for small beer. What is he, anyway?" McAlvin shrugged his shoulders and lit a cigarette. "A colonel? We could no doubt get some cute details from him. Personalities, procedures. It's interesting reading, but in this case I don't think it's worth it. Worth the time, the effort, and the money. I recommend no-go."

"Browne thinks it's worth it," Stone said. "Very much."

"This is his last run, isn't it?"

Stone looked at McAlvin, a restless, fluid man; his wiry body seemed almost boneless. He'd never been an operator in the field. He was strictly an inside man. Stone said, "Yes."

"It would be a nice coup for him," McAlvin said.

Stone turned to Bricker and Stein, sitting impassively, listening to the discussion. Bricker spoke first. "It doesn't sound high-risk to me. My reaction is, why not? Even if we got just one nugget, it would be worth it."

Stein was doubtful. "Normally, in cases of this kind, I like to go with the man in the field. So long as everything else holds up. However, in this case . . ."

"What's different about this case?" Stone asked quickly.

"It's always a temptation. . . . This is Browne's last operation. It's always a temptation to ride out on a big success. There hasn't been much happening in his area lately. Isn't that right? This is the first good news we've had from Browne in a long time. And what the hell, it's Jason's section. If Jason says he has all he needs—"

McAlvin interrupted with a wave of his hand. "You never have all you need. I merely meant to indicate there are limits."

"Well, either way. In fact, this operation sounds quite high-risk to me. High-risk versus a possible no-gain. Or no, not *no-* gain; minimum-gain. I'm a persuadable, but on the evidence so far I'm inclined to counsel no-go."

Stone turned to Carmichael, who had said nothing. Carmichael was the youngest man in the room by ten years, an economist by training; he was the director's man. "Bill?"

Carmichael said, "I'd like to hear what Browne says on the radio."

Stone had been aware of the white light blinking on his telephone. He picked up the receiver and tucked it into his chin, his mouth a quarter of an inch from the perforated black plastic. He heard her low laugh and then his name with a question mark. He said nothing. "I love you," she said at last and hung up. He waited a few moments before replacing the phone. In ten minutes Browne would come on circuit.

She turned away from the bedside table and walked downstairs to the kitchen to make another cup of coffee. That evil secretary of his; it had taken her five minutes to get by the secretary. "Is Mr. Stone in?" "Who is calling, please?" "Miss Morris." "He's in a meeting right now, Miss Morris." "Oh, my. A meeting." "I'm sorry." "I just wanted a very quick word with him." Silence. "It wouldn't take more than half a minute." "He'll be out of the meeting at noon." "But it is important." Silence. "Very." "One moment please," the secretary said, and put her on hold. Finally the connection was made, and she heard him breathing. She'd watched him talk on the telephone a thousand times and could see him now, his eyes focused elsewhere as he listened. He didn't say *anything*, that was typical. She'd asked him about that once and he'd apologized and explained that it was part of his telephone technique; he hated telephones, and when he used them, he thought of the old down-east expression: Better to close your mouth and be thought a fool than open it and remove all doubt. She did not understand how that pertained to her, *them;* but she'd let it go. He was very attentive in other ways. If he did not choose to be attentive on the telephone, that was all right. Still, a word now and again; a word wouldn't have hurt. She prepared a cup of instant and turned on the FM. Bach, they were playing Bach. The rhythmic logic of Bach enchanted her. She smiled to herself, then laughed out loud.

Browne's voice came from the receiver evenly and naturally. It was as if they were in the same room. He spoke for only five minutes, a complete report, concise and informative, no wasted words.

Stone looked around the room, satisfied. "Comment?"

Otto asked, "No doubts about authenticity?"

Browne's voice sounded a trifle bored. "None."

"And everything is laid on?"

"To a T," Browne said.

They were all silent a moment, watching each other. It was apparent that Browne had covered all the bases. Then Jason McAlvin cleared his throat. "One question. I didn't understand from your . . . presentation. How did he come to you?"

"He approached us. It was strictly over the transom, out of the blue. No cleverness on our part," he said disarmingly.

McAlvin said, "I know that. I know that, it was in the preliminary report. I mean exactly *how*. How the approach was made. And to whom."

"To a girl who works here in the embassy."

"Ah," McAlvin said. He paused, waiting for Browne to continue. But the radio was silent. McAlvin smiled. "Well, if it isn't demanding too much. One wouldn't want to pry," he said archly. "But where. When. And how."

Browne said, "Three days ago. In a café. A note. It's all quite genuine."

"And what is the girl's name?"

"She works for me," Browne said. Then he was silent again.

"Is that generally known? That she works for you?"

"I suppose the other side knows it," Browne said.

"The plot thickens," McAlvin said. He was doodling on his yellow pad, a series of connected boxes. He was carefully inking in each box.

Stone thought it was time to cut this off. McAlvin was making mischief, as usual. Stone switched off the receiver so the six of them could talk among themselves. "In what way does the plot thicken, Jason?"

"Well, these are facts I hadn't known. I thought our man had made a normal approach to one of the embassy officers. I hadn't known it was made to Browne's . . . secretary. Or whoever she is, Browne wasn't exactly precise. That changes the bidding, don't you think? He knew who she was, obviously he knows who Browne is."

"Be a damned poor intelligence man if he didn't," Stone said irritably. "He's a colonel of intelligence. That's the sort of information he'd have as a matter of course, for Christ's sake."

"Well, yes. . . ."

"He made an approach to his opposite number. Not to Browne directly; he knows that Browne's watched. That would have been obvious and dangerous. So he goes to his secretary."

"Yes, indeed," McAlvin said. "That's slightly less dangerous than going to Browne himself."

Stone switched on the receiver and turned to McAlvin. "Put the question to Browne."

"We were talking here," McAlvin said suavely. "Why do you suppose the approach was made to your secretary? Isn't that a bit dangerous? Or stupid?"

Browne said, "It all seems quite straightforward to me. A classic approach, no surprises. It seems to me"—his voice showed signs of impatience, Stone thought—"that the authenticity can easily be established by you people there. Once we have the bird in hand. My assignment is to pick him up and get him out of the country. Which I am prepared to do. And give you my evaluation of his worth, which I am also prepared to do; have done, in fact. Let me go over the salient points again. . . ."

"With all the details of the approach, please," said McAlvin.

The radio was silent; Stone knew that Browne was waiting for some sign or signal. Perhaps some sign of support. Stone said, "Proceed."

"The approach was made on the fifth of May. The girl, whose name is Chris DuPage, has a coffee in the same café every morning at nine. . . ."

Stone was listening carefully; there was something new in Browne's voice. It was something irregular. He could hear it even through the scrambling and the metallic quality of radio transmission. There was a tone and timbre he couldn't identify. Browne was being too casual. Stone knew the approach had been made through the girl; it was not unusual, though it was risky. This was Browne's girl, the one he intended to bring back with him. She was a very solid girl; Stone had known her for years. He listened to Browne talk, and suddenly something else forced its way into Stone's mind. It was a hunch from nowhere, one question, just one, and when Browne had finished, Stone asked it. "Had they ever met before?"

"Not to my knowledge," Browne said slowly.

Stone was silent a moment, along with the others. He knew what that meant. It was lawyers' talk, and not responsive. Stone looked at the radio speaker, his expression betraying nothing. He said, "We'll get back to you." Browne started to protest, but Stone didn't wait for him to finish. He switched off the radio. The operation was dead. "We'll get back to you" meant no-go.

"What happened today?" She asked the question playfully, not expecting an answer. To questions about his work he seldom answered her in any responsive way. Of course, she knew what he did but had no idea whatever how he did it or what was involved. She had no idea of the details of his professional life. But this time he surprised her.

"I had to kill one of Browne's operations."

"Brownie? But I thought he was on his way back."

"He is; this was his last job."

"What was it?"

"A defector. He'd picked up a defector."

She was astonished; he'd never disclosed so much before. Living with Stone was a continual surprise. More as a lark than anything else she decided to press him. "Why did you have to kill it?"

He shrugged and sipped his drink. "Brownie trimmed on me; he'd never done that before. There was no alternative, none at all. The thing began to smell. All you need is a whiff in an operation like that. One whiff, and you kill it."

"You caught a whiff," she said. "How?"

"Instinct." He lit a cigarette.

She looked at him. "Instinct?"

"Besides, this was just a marginal operation. It wasn't as if we were about to snatch Castro. This was just a"—he hesitated, smiling slightly —"third-level character. A bureaucrat. Useful to have, but far from necessary. Not necessary at all."

"Well," she said. She leaned toward him and plucked his cigarette from the ashtray and took a long drag. "Well, why did it smell?"

He said, "That's complicated."

She laughed, knowing he'd fall silent now. She had all she was going to get. From now on he'd turn every question with a joke, and finally change the conversation altogether. That was his habit. She said, "All the better. I like complicated stories."

"Well, it turns out that the contact was Chris. I knew that, but this morning I found out that she'd known him before. Known the defector. God knows how, or in what capacity. I *didn't* know that, and I should've known. Brownie should have told me. He didn't, and there was a reason behind that. The reason doesn't matter. It was enough that he withheld the information. That was enough to kill the operation."

She was fascinated and wanted to respond in such a way as to keep him talking. "But . . . it might have been innocent."

"I'm sure it was," Stone said.

"But if it was innocent . . . ?"

"He withheld, that was reason enough. Innocent or sinister, it makes no difference."

"You didn't *ask* him?" She was incredulous. He and Brownie had been friends for ten years. On the job and off it. They were as close as brothers.

"No. No point to that."

They were sitting on the back porch of Stone's house. He refilled their glasses with ice and tonic and stood looking into the garden. The roses were doing very nicely. They covered the board fence and drooped down to the flat bricks. He cultivated three varieties of roses, and one of the varieties was always blooming in the spring and summer.

She looked at him a moment, puzzled, not speaking. Then: "You really didn't ask him what it was about?"

"No, of course not. He'll be back here next month. I can ask him then."

"But the operation . . ."

"That's dead in any case."

She thought, What a strange world he lived in. A whiff of trouble. An "operation" abruptly "dead." No reconsideration. "In any case." He seemed to give no more thought to it than to the gin and tonic he was drinking. "Instinct," she said. "You said it was instinct. Is that all it is?"

"Informed by experience," he said dryly.

"And the experience . . ."

He said, "Informed by instinct."

She laughed, moving closer to him. "Oh, that's very helpful. May I quote that, Mr. Stone?" She looked at him a moment, wondering whether to pursue. No, that was useless. She was amazed that he'd told her as much as he had. On the other hand, she knew them both, Browne and the girl. She and Stone had seen a lot of them in the old days. The girl, Chris, had been particularly kind. "Was Chris trying to pull . . . something funny?"

"I don't know. I doubt it. You know her better than I do. What do you think?"

"I can't imagine," she said. "Chris was always careful in her work. Devoted to Brownie. I can't imagine her . . ." She let the sentence hang. "It'll be nice having them back here, won't it?"

"Yes," Stone said.

"Well," she said. "Thanks for telling me."

He said, "Thanks for the phone call."

"You didn't say anything."

"I was in a meeting."

"Well, you could've said, 'Thanks.' Or, 'Me, too.' Or just anything."

"I should've, you're right."

She said, "I feel lonely in the mornings. After you've gone to work. It's nice to hear your voice, I like it. . . ." She told him then about the day she'd had, cleaning the house, talking to a friend on the telephone; two invitations for dinner, a doctor's appointment. Then in the afternoon she lay down for a nap and had a bad dream. She almost never dreamed in the afternoon, and that upset her. It was her old dream about walking up a ramp to an airplane, the ramp becoming longer and longer in front of her eyes. The stewardess beckoning. She shook her head and reached for his cigarette; it was a very scary dream. She had tried to call him again, but he was out of his office. The dream frightened her, and she had stayed in her room until he'd come home. She had a headache. . . .

He looked at her, nodding sympathetically. He thought, What was there about him that attracted unhappy women?

D.

The hot weather affected her badly and finally she collapsed. For a month or more she'd felt edgy and distracted, and one afternoon all of her defenses crumbled at once.

A friend found her weeping in bed and called an army ambulance to take her to a private hospital on the outskirts of the capital. After a brief examination the doctor diagnosed exhaustion and melancholia and ordered her to bed for a week. He gave the head nurse prescriptions for half a dozen vitamins and drugs, including two potent tranquilizers. He did not inform the patient that he was giving her tranquilizers because he suspected that she did not believe in them. There was no direct evidence for this—just a doctor's intuition. He told the nurse to keep a close watch on the girl because he thought she might be approaching a nervous breakdown. He was not entirely sure of his ground and stressed that a breakdown was only one of several possibilities, and that if it came, it would be due as much to physical causes as mental ones. The girl was really very run-down.

The doctor explained all this to the friend, the young man who'd found her and summoned the ambulance. He omitted the part about the breakdown on the theory that it was personal and that the friend did not need to know about it. It was no more than a doctor's supposition, anyway. "She doesn't take care of herself, that's obvious," the doctor said. "It's important to do that here, in this climate. The food, the water. We'll put some vitamins in her. How old is she?"

"Twenty-six, I think. I don't know that vitamins are her problem, however. She chews vitamins like candy, a dozen pills a day. Her faith in vitamins is unshakable. Do you think it's serious?"

"I don't think so. I think she's exhausted. How's her mood been?"

"Depressed," the man said. "Everyone's depressed."

"*Tiens,*" the doctor said with a grin.

The man smiled, warming to him a little. "Sorry, I don't speak French. Your English is excellent. Idiomatic."

"I learned it in the United States," the doctor said. "My father was a diplomat." The doctor had attended medical school in Washington when his father was political counselor in the French embassy. Later the father was sent to Indochina as an adviser to the French general staff. "We were here in the early days of the war, and when they threw out the French administration, he went and I stayed." The doctor waved his hand—a weary gesture embracing the countryside, any of the anonymous communities outside the hospital compound. "They have no prejudice against doctors," he said.

The man nodded, politely, and moved as if to go. He did not want to listen to another personal history, and he'd taken a three-hour chunk out of his workday. "Well, is there anything more I can do?"

"Bring her books and magazines, things she enjoys. Not many visitors, though. Is she married? I suppose not. Being here."

"No, not married. She's unattached."

"How depressed was she?"

The man was standing in the doorway, looking at his watch. "I think she was pretty depressed, Doctor. She's been here for two years and was set to go home, and then she signed up for another tour on the spur of the moment. That was last month, and she's been understandably depressed about it ever since. She knows now that it was a mistake —everyone told her so at the time. But she doesn't like to make mistakes. Nobody does."

"Do you both work in the embassy?"

"No. She's a photographer. I work in the embassy. She free-lances pictures—she's very well known. You've probably heard of her. She signs her pictures 'D.' Everyone calls her just 'D.' Well, I must go."

"I see," said the doctor with a flicker of a smile.

"I'll look in later," the man said, and was gone.

The hospital was not air-conditioned, and all the windows were thrown open to the hot weather. Because the buildings were situated under large shade trees, the rooms were really quite comfortable. Slowly turning ceiling fans moved the still air.

D.'s room was large, and from the window next to her bed she looked out over a wide lawn with narrow hedges, and benches where the patients sat. She'd always meant to do a picture story on the hospital. The patients were mostly American civilians. There were a few French and an occasional local, if the local was rich enough to afford the fees or too important to be turned away. The hospital was adequately equipped and decently maintained, and it was always assumed there was a subsidy of some kind, probably from American Intelligence. There were rumors that the doctors occasionally treated important enemy cadre as a hedge against sabotage or extortion. But that was nowhere proved except in the negative: it was a fact that the hospital had never been touched in any way by the war and existed as an island of neutrality, a collection of anonymous buildings on the outskirts of the capital.

The first day in the hospital D. slept for eighteen hours straight, but when she awoke she felt no better. Her skin was clammy to the touch and she was shaky. She felt robbed of her energy and ten years older and she didn't know what was wrong. She explained this to the doctor, who listened attentively but said nothing to relieve her mind.

"Look at my fingers," she insisted. She held her hands out, palms down, and they watched the slender fingers tremble.

The doctor raised his eyebrows but said nothing.

"I feel like that on the inside too. Particularly my stomach. My appetite's shot. Oh, damn," she said brokenly. "Sometimes I feel like crying. I feel like crying right now, for no reason. Damn, I hate it so."

"It's all right. There's no law against it."

She smiled thinly. "You mean you give your permission? I can cry right now with no loss of face?"

The doctor perched on the edge of her bed and took her wrist in his hand to check her pulse. His expression was very serious. "I think I might even prescribe it."

"Oh, a good cry. Let the little lady have a good cry—right?"

"If she wants," the doctor said, looking at her squarely for the first time. He was concentrating on her pulse, which seemed steady.

She smiled, looking at his fingers on her wrist. She thought he was probably nicer than he sounded. "You mean I can cry right now?"

"Absolutely."

"Well, I guess I will." The girl laughed and began to cry. Large tears rolled down her cheeks and hesitated on her chin. She made no sound. She turned her face to the wall. With her free hand she covered her eyes.

"Your friend told me you were a photographer." He watched her head nod slowly. She was not crying now but her face was still turned away. "You're very well known. I should've heard of you."

"Top of the trade," the girl said matter-of-factly. "I photograph for a lot of French magazines. *Match.* And *Elle.* Also the French *Vogue.*"

"It's been years since I've seen *Elle,*" the doctor said.

"You don't know what you're missing."

"Yes I do."

She dropped her hand from her eyes and looked at him. He still had her wrist in his fingers and was counting.

"Before I came over here I was a fashion photographer. There aren't very many women fashion photographers. Most of my assignments were taking pictures of men."

"That's very unusual," he said. Her pulse was irregular now.

"Well, that's what I do here too. Take pictures of men. My picture file, a couple of thousand snaps of green men. Men dressed in green. Long, short, tall, and all of them green. They're like plants wilting in the heat. They all wilt sooner or later. Think of it—a thousand pictures plus. I have a snap for every conceivable occasion. I send them to my agent in New York, and when news magazines are doing a spread they can select the pictures they need. The pictures are all there on file, so an editor has only to taxi across town and go through the file cabinet. By the way, that's green too."

She was silent for a moment, and the doctor thought that she had fallen asleep. He released her wrist and stood up, appraising the small figure in the bed. But her head turned and she looked at him, tears still in the corners of her eyes, wide awake now.

"Why don't you come later and we can have a drink before dinner? A glass of wine—isn't that supposed to be good for the spirits? It's just a bore, being here alone. I think my friend brought me some white wine."

He was looking at her, no longer thinking of her pulse. "I can be back at six."

"Don't forget."

"I won't forget. Would you like some cheese?"

"The cheese in this country is terrible."

"You'll like mine," the doctor said. "I have a private source of supply."

"All right—wine and cheese. And I'll tell you more about my snaps."

The doctor laughed and wrinkled up his face in an exaggerated grimace. "I can hardly wait," he said.

He liked her. She reminded him of his daughter in France. D. was twenty-six, eight years older than his daughter, but they had the same assured outlook on life. Very dry and beautifully made, D. could have been a fashion model herself except that she was petite. But she had a startling, direct look to her, and large brown eyes that seemed to take in everything. It did not surprise him that she was a photographer. The doctor thought that she was in no way frail, which made the facts of her illness all the more puzzling.

The preliminary tests were inconclusive—a high white-cell count and an irregular pulse, temperature a steady ninety-nine degrees. The doctor thought she was suffering from a low-grade infection of some kind, complicated by simple exhaustion. She was underweight and her eyes were too bright and her skin was dull. With all this she maintained a kind of bravado—as if her vitality were merely in hiding and at any moment would reappear.

On the evening of her fourth day in the hospital he decided to tell her he could not diagnose her illness. He couldn't make a positive diagnosis of a physical problem. He'd assembled symptoms, not causes.

"I thought at first you were having a nervous breakdown. I don't think that anymore, although you're obviously upset. I shouldn't be telling you this, really, but perhaps if you knew it yourself . . ." His voice trailed off. "What makes it puzzling to me is that you're not a neurotic."

She smiled because he pronounced the word with a French accent —noo-row-teak. "How do you know that?"

"Hunch."

"Well, you're right."

"It was your attitude."

"Well, the pills aren't helping any. I don't feel any different when I take them."

He said, "No, I can see that."

She was propped up in bed, her drink balanced on her knees.

"Have you ever thought about going home? Back to America?"

"What's a nice girl like you doing in a place like this?"

"Exactly."

"This place, it's a cliché. I couldn't say anything you'd believe, and you'd be right for not believing it. It's embarrassing for me to say, it's so dumb." She waited for him to answer but he said nothing. "Well, it's part of our time, isn't it? Where else would one want to be? While this was going on and you were a photographer, would you want to be photographing models for a fashion magazine?" She raised her eyebrows and shuddered, laughing. "Besides, I just extended my contract. This is a binding contract, although obviously if I stay sick, I'll have to go home. I'm counting on you to prevent that. I've never reneged on a contract. In my work you have respect for contracts and for deadlines. And it doesn't matter that I've already been here on and off for two years. That doesn't matter a bit—no Brownie points for that. I've signed a contract with a magazine and I intend to stick by it."

The doctor was amused. He wondered what it was about Americans and their contracts. One dedicates and defines one's life for a piece of paper. Signed by oneself. It offended his sense of logic and brought to mind the cheap patriotic talk of politicians. He thought it would be simpler for this girl to acknowledge her feelings of guilt.

D. said, "This war is the opiate of the people."

He snorted.

She laughed in spite of herself. The doctor was having none of it. Well, there was no reason why he should.

"You ought to withdraw," he said. "Kick the habit."

"I will if you will," she said. "You who've been here—how long?"

"Eighteen years."

"Well. Fancy that."

"You remind me of me," he said after a moment. "That's what I did the first year I was here. I signed up, and then I signed up again. I had a different answer for every person who asked me why. Before I knew it, I'd been here five years. The sixth year, my wife took my daughter and left. Later I was supposed to meet her in the South of France. But it never happened. I acquired a financial interest in this place. One thing and another. I've been here all these years. This hospital."

"Are you glad?"

"Glad? I never thought of it that way."

"Well, are you sorry you didn't follow your wife?"

"No—that was over. She married a dentist a few years after arriving back in France. She's happy, the child's happy. There wasn't much of a life for them here."

"But you. There was a life for you," she said, pressing him.

"Of course."

"I can't conceive of living here with a family."

The doctor smiled. "Neither could my wife."

She balanced the wineglass on her knee and frowned. She said, "I was living with a man here, but he left. Now, that was odd because it happened without warning—usually there's a warning signal. One morning he announced he'd had it in the war zone and was going home and to hell with the consequences. He worked for a research outfit, very hush-hush. There was something in his contract about mental stress and strain. He copped a plea on that and they sent him home. He was here one day and gone the next. I drove him to the airport and he promised to write but he never did."

"You didn't follow?"

She looked at him a long moment, surprised and irritated. "Of course not."

"Sounds a little like my wife. One morning she announced that the country was going to hell and she didn't intend to go to hell with it. She was very *French*—do you know what I mean by that? She was seriously chic and enjoyed conversation. She liked to travel. She liked to shop—"

The girl giggled and touched his hand. "Isn't that funny? I haven't been shopping in a year. *Shopping*—that was something my mother did. I haven't bought a dress in a year. I don't own a hat except for my steel pot. I haven't bought any jewelry in two years and I can't imagine buying any ever. I bought a Nikon in Hong Kong, but that was business. *Shopping*. That's a scream. Why, I don't even collect half my income. It's banked for me in New York."

". . . so I booked her on Air France to Paris and she was gone in a week, furniture to follow. I didn't see her or my daughter for a year and a half because we were very busy then and I couldn't leave the country. One has responsibilities. So I stayed, and my wife remarried."

"I remember, now that I think about it, that six months ago I bought a cashmere sweater in Hong Kong."

"A few years ago I lived with a woman who sang in one of the nightclubs. But she tired of the life here, too, and left. She made quite a good income before leaving. She was very careful with money. Of all the women I've known here, she was the most agreeable."

All this was said intently and swiftly, the words bright with nostalgia and amusement. They spoke as if time were running out on them and they had to get everything said at once. Their voices were low and intimate, their eyes focused elsewhere. Now they were silent, sipping wine and watching the darkness come. From somewhere on the hospital floor they heard rapid steps, and then it was silent again.

The doctor said, "In this country one does not lack for people." At times he felt the country was like a waiting room in a clinic. It was a place where people came to pause and wait but never to live. Never to put down roots. He imagined a faded waiting room with run-down décor and out-of-date magazines, the walls soiled, the floor scuffed.

"I was going out with a colonel, but his tour ended and they sent him home. He's at some base in the States now. Nice man. There was the colonel, the researcher, and one other who's still here. That one just *ended*, bang." She waited for a reply, some exchange.

"One becomes caught up," he said.

"One does."

He raised his glass and smiled. "Regrets are awfully damp, don't you think?"

She shook her head, waving his words away with a flick of her wrist. "Oh, no. I have no regrets. Why should I have regrets? I'm twenty-six; I enjoy my work here. I don't *love* it, as some of them do, but I think it's important and I like to do it. I'm good, by the way. My friends in New York thought it was a lark when I came here. '*Vogue* goes to the war'—that kind of thing. They all thought it was just another lark, but it wasn't." She was silent a moment, remembering things her friends had said about her. "I found that once I was here, I had to stay on." She smiled sardonically. "And that had nothing to do with the contract."

"It's easier to stay than to go—that's the diabolical thing. And it gets easier the longer you're here." He was conscious of sounding like the voice of experience, middle-aged and world-weary, almost cynical.

"For a while I lived at the hotel, but then I got a flat. I decorated the place and that may have been a mistake—temple rubbings, bronze Buddhas. Our equivalent of college pennants, I suppose. But it's home and it's convenient, and I'm attached to it."

He nodded, understanding what she was saying. He'd lived in a hotel for two years following his divorce. As a transient he could work himself to exhaustion. He was working eighteen hours a day until one murderous afternoon when three of his patients died on the operating table and he walked into the waiting room and saw twenty more. He understood then that there would never be enough hours in the day to care for all the casualties, and that evening he checked out of the hotel and found himself a small flat in a quiet neighborhood. Now he worked from sunup to sunset, only vaguely bothered by his atrophied ability. (He had no time to read the truly advanced medical journals, and it had been years since he'd been inside a first-rate hospital.) When the sun went down he went home. If there were patients in the waiting room, they were told to come back tomorrow. Sundays he worked on the hospital accounts.

He asked her, "Do you take days off?"

She looked at him strangely. "Well, not often. Every three or four months I take a vacation. But when I'm here I work. I hustle. There are more pictures here than I can ever take."

It was dusk and patients were strolling in the park. They wore blue smocks and clogs and strolled in twos and threes around the gravel paths. They walked very slowly, as sick people do. It was quiet outside, the light failing behind the shade trees, indistinct shadows reaching across the lawn. A soft breeze stirred the curtain. The doctor had had too much wine and felt light-headed. He'd intended to return to his office to check X rays and then meet a colleague for dinner. But he'd stayed on, talking to the girl, fascinated by her and wary of her at the same time. He'd stayed with her while she ate her supper, discreetly moving to the window when the nurse came at seven to clear the tray and give her an alcohol rubdown. Now it was eight, and he was tired and hungry and no longer sober.

"I must go," the doctor said.

"No, please don't."

"It's late. I've X rays."

"We're having such a good time. Are you sad, all this talk about the past?"

"No," he lied.

"It's like a reminiscence. Only a little bit damp. I like it. I like it that we connect and it's not necessary to spell everything out."

"Yes and no," he said. He finished the last of his wine, thinking about the singer, the one who had come and gone. She had been very careful with her money, not so careful with his.

"This hospital. It's yours, isn't it?"

"Only partly. It's owned by a group—most of them are French."

"But you're the head man." She looked at him, smiling. "You know there are rumors. I've heard that you treat enemy in here. Important enemy, wounded or whatever and unable to get back to their own base hospitals. You treat them anyway, the same as anyone else. Me."

"A charming story," the doctor said.

"And true."

"No comment, *rien,* " he said, laughing. "This is an ordinary hospital. We have nothing to do with the military authorities."

"I can see that."

"We heal whoever comes to our door."

"I believe it." She was thinking that she would do the picture story when she got out of the hospital. But it would be necessary to get snaps of them actually in the operating room. It would make a dandy story, quite a coup. She wondered if she could talk the doctor into it. "Let me photograph it sometime," she said playfully.

"Yes, the next time General Giap comes in for a tonsillectomy I'll tell him you're here. D. from *Vogue. Vogue* wants to do a cover story on you, *mon général.* D. wants you in your fatigues and then in your black pajamas on the operating table." He began to laugh.

She protested, "I was joking!"

"No more jokes," he said. "You see the problem?"

"Yes-I-see-the-problem."

"I think you need another week here—seriously."

"I suppose so." She was no longer thinking about the picture story, concentrating instead on staying awake. She was drowsy from the wine and lulled by the doctor's voice.

"You're exhausted. I know you've been working too hard. It would not surprise me if you were working right now. You're depressed and it's had its effect on your body. All these things are connected. . . ."

"Yes, *Doctor.*" She did not feel depressed at all.

He smiled, knowing she found his bedside manner ludicrous. "You've been shaken up—you move around too much. You'll be all right, but you need rest. Sleep."

"I've been sleeping for a week," she murmured. Then, softly: "I'm having such a good time."

"It's as good as any place."

"Better."

He fell silent. It was awkward for him. He'd lived alone for so long, living in his work. The hospital rooms were as familiar as the rooms of his own flat. He knew their dimensions, the look of them at different hours of the day; those he'd slept in, those he hadn't. There'd been so many sick and wounded. This girl was not dangerously ill, only run-down and depressed; her nerve was fine.

"You're enchanting," he said in French, so softly that he was certain she could not hear. He didn't want her to think him foolish. The situation was banal. If anything was to happen, he wanted it to happen naturally, with no forcing. He repeated several other phrases in French to himself.

She looked at him and smiled. She moved toward him and put her cheek in his open palm. She felt his rough skin and kissed his wrist. He wore a battered brass bracelet that had turned his skin green and smelled like an old penny. She wrinkled her nose and pushed it back and forth on his wrist. She pressed his hand close to her cheek, and he bent down and caressed her hair with his lips. Then he had her face in both his hands, holding it lightly as he would a child's. His hands trembled slightly, but he did nothing to correct or disguise their tremor. His eyes shut tight, he put his face next to hers, very carefully so that his beard would not scratch her. He tried to erase his memory, to force the past from it. He wanted to live in the present as she did. They stayed like that a full minute, and when the doctor got up to leave it was all he could do to take his hand away from her skin. In a daze he leaned over and kissed her, hearing her gentle breathing.

"Tomorrow night," she said.

He smiled at her, nodding slightly.

"You're so good."

And you, he said in French.

"Please stay. Stay with me here." Her speech was slurred.

He shook his head and told her she was almost asleep as it was. She needed sleep. He'd be back in the morning—eight o'clock, as always.

She raised herself on one arm and brushed the hair from her forehead. "I want to ask you just one thing. Just one—something silly. Will you tell me? You won't hold anything back?"

He nodded, encouraged by the expression in her eyes.

"What kind of drugs are these?" She held up two bottles. "They aren't vitamins. They're bitter and they're the wrong size."

He said, "They help you sleep. They're harmless. Don't worry about them. I sometimes use them myself."

"They're tranquilizers, aren't they?"

He nodded.

She handed him both bottles and shook her head firmly, a quick shudder. She said, "No tranquilizers. Take them back. Give them to someone who needs them. No offense—there was no way you could've known. But I don't want *them.*"

He accepted the bottles. Both were more than half full; she could not have taken more than a couple of pills. He stood by the door, looking at her; she was flushed and smiling and determined in the big bed. She glanced away, her hand touching her cheek. She was almost asleep. He put the bottles in his pocket and backed out the door, still looking at her. In the hallway he paused and slumped against the wall, so tired, smiling privately and thinking to himself in French. The girl was formidable, a treasure. He looked back at the door, closed now. No, she didn't need tranquilizers. She didn't need them now. He'd understood that from the beginning. His doctor's intuition was exquisite, as always. So young—her vitality was returning; she'd be well in a week, and off to photograph her multitudes of green men. He shook his head sadly. What a run they could have had.

PART III

Cease-fire

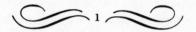

At the end of the day we gathered in McDonough's room. The games of bridge began in his air-conditioned sitting room, then moved to the balcony when the sun went down. From McDonough's balcony we could see all the points of interest, the embassy and the Presidential Palace and the lately abandoned United Nations Command Post. The games lasted for an hour or for eight hours, depending on the way the cards fell. Dummy was expected to watch the city below, looking for suspicious traffic and listening for sudden noise. But the island was quiet. The cease-fire was holding, thanks to McDonough and me.

We played bridge on a wrought-iron table on the balcony, and when the game was interesting McDonough would call room service and we would eat in. We were tired and had lost the taste for long hours in the hotel bar and late, muddled meals with the ladies and gentlemen of the press. At the table were McDonough and me, General Grandoni, and the general's aide-de-camp, a Pole named Molz. We drank beer or lemonade, complained about the weather, and discussed the situation on the island. McDonough turned up the volume on Brahms and we spoke softly, in German so Molz could understand. We four got on fairly well, everyone wanted to see the negotiations succeed so we could leave the island. Even Molz was cooperative.

Grandoni was the Secretary-General's personal representative. He and McDonough met with the combatants every afternoon. Molz was present as amanuensis. I was the inside man, verifying the violations and interpreting the protocol. In the beginning we were a team of twenty specialists and a battalion of Yugoslav troops, the peace-keeping force. But now there were just the four of us, Grandoni the chairman, McDonough the negotiator, and I the lawyer. Molz had no function, but he was a Communist and it was important that the delegation be balanced. In the evenings around the bridge table we would discuss the afternoon's meeting and set an agenda for the next day. Grandoni, Molz with him like a shadow, would leave for the Swiss embassy at seven to cable a message to the Secretary-General. Then, alone, McDonough and I would decide between us what would be done the next day; the words McDonough would use and in what order and with what inflections. We made an odd pair, McDonough and Irish radical and I a pragmatic American. However, he was more radical than Irish and I was more American than pragmatic.

Radical, in the sense that he went to the roots of things. He was the least self-deluded man I have ever known, and it is no contradiction to add that he was a romantic in his own fashion, a high-bouncing lover and patron of the arts. McDonough accompanied me sometimes to the small museum near the marketplace. I took tea with the curator most days in the late afternoon, finding him valuable in a number of unexpected ways. He was an anthropologist and enjoyed retailing legends of the island's glorious past. He wished us success in our negotiations but doubted that anything permanent could be achieved. He believed that his island was cursed, a concept that appealed to Ned. One afternoon on impulse I gave him a personal check for three hundred dollars. For the new dig, I said. Smiling bleakly, murmuring thanks, the curator tucked the check away in his vest pocket. Magnanimous, Ned said when we left. What do you think that'll get you? A ticket out of here? Is it a talisman? I nodded. That was exactly what I thought, or hoped.

I amused myself in the early mornings by writing lengthy letters to my wife, describing my colleagues and the atmosphere on the island. Two weeks ago I did something I have never done, with my wife or with anyone else. I wrote her a long pornographic letter. Diana, surprised but game, tried to reply in kind but her letter was clumsy and self-conscious and at the end she appended a postscript, news of the children. Then yesterday she called and said it was time I demanded to be relieved; six weeks was too long and the island was now quiet. She said she was better in the flesh, which was true, and that she and the children were lonely without me. I warned her that one did not "demand" anything from Nicolo de Grandoni, count, patriot, warrior, and personal representative of the Secretary-General. General Grandoni followed instructions to the letter and we four would remain on the island until the assignment was concluded. Probably four more weeks, I told her. But why didn't she come for a long weekend? No, no, she said; that was impossible. She asked me why McDonough couldn't do what I did. I began to laugh because I'd told her a little of McDonough's temperament. I said, Not a chance.

That night at eight the general returned from the Swiss embassy, mustaches bristling, with the news that he'd spoken personally to the Secretary-General at a golf club in the county of Westchester. He, Grandoni, was to return immediately to New York. I was to return to my base in London. The feeling inside the secretariat was that our mission should be downgraded, "made inconspicuous" and therefore an encouraging sign to the combatants. McDonough began to laugh but Grandoni silenced him with a look. "You and Molz are to remain," Grandoni said. "Indefinitely," he added maliciously. Molz sat with a satisfied expression, examining his boots. After a few more words Grandoni and Molz departed.

I saluted McDonough with the glass of lemonade and he began to chortle softly. He was sitting with his feet on the balcony railing, looking into the square below. He picked up his discards and began to sail them, one by one, into the night. "Dumbest damn thing I ever heard of, in forty-eight hours this place will explode. Again." He continued to pitch the cards over the balcony. "Now what am I supposed to do? With you gone I'll have to take up womanizing again. As an alternative to gin rummy with Molz. It's disgusting."

I said, "Remember that girl—"

"Sonia," McDonough said. "And she's gone. I checked."

I had not been thinking of Sonia. "Sonia was trouble."

"Ned McDonough would rather die of trouble than die of boredom." The last of the cards flew into the night and McDonough slapped his palms, satisfied. I stood and looked over the balcony. No one was in the square but a few of the cards were still floating in the thick night air. "Well," I said. "We did good work."

"Not so bad."

"We did very good work the first three weeks."

"Once we shook Comrade Molz," McDonough amended. "We made a hell of a team."

I said, "I'm not anxious to spend another minute here. But this is premature. They've made a mistake. And it's a pain in the ass for you—"

He shrugged, gazing across the darkened square. "It's no matter to me whether I stay for another week or another month. Weeks, months; it's all the same to me. I'd just as soon be here as anywhere." We both smiled. "And it'll be interesting even so, even with Molz. Maybe especially with Molz."

"I'm glad to be going," I said bluntly. He asked me if I were laying over in Athens and I said I was. There was a long wait between planes. I was impatient to get to my room and pack. If I caught the midnight plane to Athens I could be in London by tomorrow evening. McDonough smiled strangely and reached into his desk and brought out a single key on a silver chain. "You can have my flat for the night. No one's there. I haven't seen the place in months. I'll give you a note for the concierge and you can leave the key with her when you leave." I took the key, surprised; McDonough had said nothing about a flat in Athens. "Damn nice flat, I've had it for years." He reached for the pitcher of lemonade, then thought better of it and poured us two cognacs. The night was warm and the lemonade tepid. "Time for Ned to return to his old haunts," he said. "And it is most definitely time for a new companion." Suddenly I was sorry to leave him; I suspected that he and Molz would make a destructive combination. We sat and talked for a while and then I went to my room, packed, checked out of the hotel, and left for the airport.

Of course the flight was delayed. I sat in the airport bar, watching mechanics tinker with the landing gear of the 707. It was not a sight to inspire confidence and I was inclined to return to the hotel and take a morning plane. But I was sick of that particular Hilton, it seemed to me that I'd spent half my life in Hilton hotels. Men do travel in diverse ways. I have a friend who takes an attaché case containing nothing but personal effects from his bedroom at home. This friend believes that if he duplicates his own bedroom in a hotel he will be less tense and lonely, and perhaps he is; he says he is. I travel with three suitcases of clothes, though I think of my trips as interregnums; they are parentheses in my life (though my wife believes the reverse). The particular work that I do is specialized and technical and requires concentration and I would rather not be reminded of Diana and the children and my house in St. John's Wood. I bring nothing personal except my worn copy of Walter Lippmann's *A Preface to Morals,* which I read when I become discouraged. It is really about politics, not morals, as indicated by the title to the first chapter: "Whirl Is King." On the road I tend to be all business, except at those times when I encounter men like McDonough. Thank God it isn't often, they're magnets to men like me. Laughter and excitement follow them wherever they go, or seem to, their lives buoyed by luck and privilege. In a way they resemble royalty, envied and resented by turns. The relationship is political: if McDonough were a government, he'd be overthrown. I envy his anarchic life, no possibility ignored. His life seems to me a work of art, a created thing, and I am aware that that says as much about me as it does about him. He told me once that he viewed his existence as a romance, meaning something removed from ordinary concerns, a life with no ties or duties or special loyalties to anything except himself and his work.

He'd found a girl in the bar of the hotel the first week. We called her Anne-of-the-thousand-days, an evidently rich and certainly comely heiress from Fitzgerald country who filed intermittently for the Voice of America, making the Troubles sound like a drunken lunch at Tuxedo Park. Of course she and McDonough had friends in common, and one of these turned out to be an old lover of Ned's. It was as if they'd discovered a mutual godmother, and Anne-of-the-thousand-days knew immediately that Ned would "do." The VOA recalled her after three weeks so the affair languished, though naturally they corresponded. McDonough corresponded with women everywhere, no post was satisfactory unless it brought scented letters from women. It is reasonable to suppose that this confident life had flaws; most lives do. There was after all no family and no one person he was bound to; he had made few promises; his life lacked essence. And what would happen to him when he was old? A work of art, whether portrait, sonnet, or symphony, had an end as well as a beginning: a last brushstroke, a fourteenth line or coda. Anne-of-the-thousand-days, like the others, slipped out of his life as easily as she had slipped into it. Of course I never asked him if at times, late at night, he yearned for a home and family. It would have been like asking Bakunin if really, truly, he wouldn't, honestly now, rather be a businessman. No, he would not. Would anyone? Would I?

The plane left at 3 A.M. I spent the last hour in the airport bar with one of the stewardesses, who confided to me that the difficulty was not with the landing gear but with the pilot. He had not arrived and a search was under way. But I was not to worry, this happened frequently and the delay was never more than a few hours. I replied quickly that it didn't matter to me; three hours, six hours, it was all the same. I was going home and my conscience was clear.

I did not sleep at all on the plane, and approaching Greece in a brilliant sunrise I found myself ravenously hungry. Throttling down, the plane shuddered and I watched the sunlight play on the water. Athens was a marvelous city. I reflected that my work tended to take me to second-rate countries; but there was always a first-rate city nearby. Nearly always. I had been in most of the second-rate countries of the world, and nearly all of the first-rate cities, always on business . . . organization business. Inside the terminal I paused at a newsstand to buy the papers and a magazine and a postcard, intending to send the post-card to McDonough. Then I looked at the flight schedules. The next plane for London was at noon. There were others at three and at five-thirty. I stood looking at the departure times, then went to fetch my bags. Outside, surrounded by luggage, light-headed in the early-morning coolness, I looked for the stewardess. We had agreed to share a cab downtown, she to her hotel and I to McDonough's flat. She waved from an ancient Mercedes and as we moved away from the terminal I thought suddenly that it would be wonderful to drive to the port and have breakfast, a full carte of fish and wine, a dessert, and strong coffee. I felt like celebrating; it was not a morning to sleep through. We could sit in the café under an awning and watch the boats put out to sea. The stewardess was easily convinced and I told the driver to take us to the best café at the port.

She was petite and trim in her blue skirt and white blouse and her appetite was healthy. She was not indifferent to wine and we drank two bottles of Roditis. I described my six weeks on the island, making them sound more amusing than they were. Not mentioned were the museum or the marketplace or Grandoni or Molz or Anne-of-the-thousand-days. The stories were of McDonough and me, two raffish businessmen at play. She said she hated the island, the tension at the airport; half the flights were delayed for one reason or another. I confided finally that I missed London and was happy going home. I had enjoyed the island but was anxious to return to my normal routine. In the last analysis, I said, the island's Troubles were of no lasting significance. "The situation is hopeless but not serious," I said with a smile. She smiled back. "Except for the women and children, of course," she said.

By nine we were both yawning. The sun blinded us, the waters of the harbor flashing like diamonds. I had shed my coat and tie and was sitting in shirt sleeves, sweating. The café was crowded now and we sat with our backs to the water. She looked at me and said she had to get some sleep. I paid the bill and hailed a cab, wondering whether she would come to McDonough's flat with me. Inside the cab I turned toward her but she had pulled away into the corner of the seat, her eyes closed. I stared at her a long moment, hoping her eyes would open or her face give some other sign of life. Finally I decided that negotiations would be long, complicated, and probably unsatisfactory. I touched her hand and when she stirred without reply or answering pressure I turned away, suddenly angry, believing that I had somehow been cheated, or cheated myself. My light-headedness returned when she opened the door and got out, saying good-bye with a tight smile and a polite wave. I thought it was just as well. McDonough's flat was only five minutes from her hotel.

The concierge was out and I walked up the three floors and let myself in with the key on the silver chain. The wine had made me languid and I leaned against the doorjamb, looking into Ned McDonough's deathly silent apartment. I put my bags down and listened in the darkness a moment, and then I switched on the living room lights. The room was comfortably furnished, indubitably a man's room—but that was not what astounded me. The walls of the living room and every free surface were crowded with photographs. They were photographs of McDonough, a woman of his own age, and various children, singly and together. A sideboard accommodated three photographs, and an end table four. They covered the walls, photographs of every conceivable shape and size. I moved forward in the silence, looking more closely, peering at them. I saw a handsome family at play, McDonough with his arm around a young boy on a porch swing, McDonough and the woman smiling together, their arms linked, pointing; the picture was off center, it had no doubt been taken by a child. There was McDonough and two children on a boat somewhere; McDonough holding an infant; the woman and a young girl (unmistakably mother and daughter) on a beach; a rowdy birthday party; standing with fishing rods on a wooden dock; in a loaded station wagon. There were photographs everywhere, some of them overexposed and out of focus, like those in any family album. I was dismayed because it was obvious from the first moment that this was McDonough's family, preserved in frames. I felt as if I'd been caught looking through his wallet or diary. The photographs were entirely private; excruciatingly so, for they revealed nothing to an outsider. It was like looking at a military atlas of an unfamiliar war: the outlines of the struggle were visible, the sides advanced and retreated, ground was gained and lost—but what was at stake? Who were the combatants? There was a man, his wife, and the children. The youngest boy was self-conscious. The oldest boy looked like his father. The girl was pretty like her mother. McDonough had never hinted at any of this and it was then that I remembered the peculiar smile when he'd offered me the key to his flat, not visited "in months."

I wandered into the bedroom, still feeling a trespasser. The closet was filled with men's suits and on his bureau was a formal portrait of his wife, this one obviously made by a professional. She was a tall woman with wide-set eyes and long dark hair. I turned away in confusion, then looked back at her; she had an alluring mouth. McDonough's wife was wearing a man's shirt and khaki pants and her thumbs were hooked into her belt. She was staring straight into the camera's lens. I took off my shirt and trousers and went into the bathroom, grateful that there were no photographs on the tiled walls. I stood in the shower and soaked, my thoughts muddled. I had gone from high gear to low in thirty minutes.

I decided to call Diana right away and tell her I would take the noon plane. She always met me at Heathrow.

I went straight to the telephone from the shower. The housekeeper answered after one ring. No, Mrs. Lyons was not at home. She had tried to reach me yesterday and again this morning but the Hilton did not know my whereabouts. Mrs. Lyons was concerned, it was an inconvenience. I listened to all of this with mounting irritation. At any event, the housekeeper said, my wife had received an urgent message from America. Her brother was ill and she had flown to New York to be with him. She intended to return on Monday or at midweek, depending. It was apparently not critical, but it was serious. I said nothing. Diana's brother was an invalid. Their parents were dead and brother and sister were uncommonly close. Diana and her hound, I thought bitterly. I asked how the children were and the housekeeper replied dryly that they were fine, of course; both of them were at school. I gave the housekeeper the telephone number of Ned's flat. In case Diana called home she was to relay it, please. But I would call her myself later in the day, in New York, at the clinic where her brother lived. The housekeeper asked coldly when I was returning to London. I said I'd let her know and hung up.

I looked into the kitchen and opened the refrigerator. It was well stocked, unopened tins of orange juice and a bottle of milk and plates of ham and cheese and eggs in a wire basket. *Damn,* I said aloud, remembering the stewardess and how she looked in the backseat with her eyes closed. I was breathing the iced air of the refrigerator and trying to think clearly. No point now to take the noon plane. I was tired and feeling the aftereffects of the wine, and sleeplessness. I wished I'd negotiated with the stew after all. I backed out of the kitchen and went to the window, the curtains drawn against the sun. I felt surrounded by McDonough's family, the pretty woman and the children and their life together, all of it mysterious. I thought of Ned and his suite at the Hilton, and the late-night bridge games; it seemed a world away. I pulled apart the curtains and stood looking into the street below, burning in the sun; the street was white as an eyeball and deserted. I could see my reflection in the glass and that was in no way reassuring. My face was drawn and lined and I needed a shave. No, I thought; I needed sleep. A long sleep now, and rational plans later.

Well, hell; the poor bastard. Diana's brother had polio when he was a child. His recovery was nearly complete when complications developed. Then his mother died and a month later his father was killed in an auto accident. He was thirty now and lived in a private clinic on the East Side of New York, a young man who quickly attracted sympathy and just as quickly repelled it. He possessed a sharp and savage tongue; loathing himself, cursing the cards he'd been dealt, he chose to blame his sister. He crooked his finger and Diana jumped always. And he always managed to crook his finger at rotten times.

I stood staring into the street, then shook my head and went on into McDonough's bedroom. I avoided looking at the walls or at the woman in the picture frame. I took off all my clothes and stood there a moment, my socks in my hand. Sleep, I thought; a long sleep. I muttered a brief apology to Diana for beating up on her crippled brother. The poor bastard. Then I balled one of the socks and threw it as hard as I could against the wall. It made a soft sound, *thuh,* and caught on the edge of a picture frame and hung there weakly.

The curtains in the bedroom were open a crack and, waking, I saw it was still daylight. My head hurt and I was sweating and still disoriented. I lit a cigarette and lay still for a moment. Then I heard a noise somewhere and climbed out of bed. A radio was playing very softly. I padded into the living room, where the curtains were open, admitting stark afternoon sun, creamy and hot. I followed the sound of the music into the hall and then into McDonough's narrow study. The light, so brilliant that it blinded me looking into it, came through french doors leading to a tiny balcony. The doors were open and I stood in the sunlight and looked at the girl on the balcony. She lay as if in fire, heat waves rising around her, a mirage. She lay on her stomach, her body brown except for a narrow pale stripe across her back and another across the rise of her buttocks. A transistor radio rested between her feet. She was fifteen feet away but I could see the tiny hairs in the small of her back move in the soft breeze, rising and falling with her breathing. Her head was turned away from me and the sun flashed off a pea-sized gold earring. I was slick with sweat standing in the sun but she was dry, appearing cool and fresh in the appalling heat. I stepped back into the darkness of hall and stood watching her, perfectly framed in the French doors. It was like looking at a portrait in a gallery, and wondering if by watching it you could make it come to life.

I did not know whether to advance or retreat. I had no idea who she was, except she was not the woman in McDonough's photographs. That woman was dark and big-boned and this one was slender and light. She raised her arm then and I took a quick step backward, quietly so that she wouldn't hear me. I didn't want to alarm her, she would believe that the flat was deserted. I walked into the kitchen and pulled a towel around myself and put on water for tea. Then I noticed my suitcases in the hall. It was obvious she knew that I, or someone, was there. I walked back into the study but by then she was on her feet, dressed, looking at me and grinning. She was very beautiful with the sun at her back.

I said, "Sorry."

She made a nervous gesture with her hands. "It's too hot."

"I'm making tea," I said. "We can have some iced tea." Then I put out my hand. "I'm Wylie." She murmured a name I did not catch and moved out of the light into the hallway. We both retreated into the kitchen.

She said, "I come up here sometimes after work, to lie in the sun and read."

"You're American," I said.

She made a face. "Canadian."

I smiled. Canadians were always touchy. "Well, I'm sorry."

"My mother was American. You were half right."

I turned away from her to fetch a large pitcher. I filled it with ice, then dumped four teabags into a china pot. The water was almost boiling. I got a large lemon from the refrigerator and a knife to cut it with and two tall glasses. I put the sugar next to the pitcher. She watched me fussing with these things and smiled widely. I had placed the glasses just so on the countertop and now she moved forward and with her forefinger gently touched one of them out of line. She had the smallest hands I have ever seen.

"Do you work with Ned?"

I said, "Sometimes." The water was boiling and I poured it into the pot. We stood a moment, ill at ease, not speaking, watching the pot. Without thinking, I moved the glass back into line.

She said, "I'll turn on the air conditioning." I followed her into the study. It was so hot I imagined the books melting on their shelves, a library by Dali. She brought the radio from the balcony, closing the French doors and drawing the curtains. Then she moved behind the leather chair and turned on a window unit. Presently I felt cool air begin to circulate in the darkened room. She dropped onto the couch and I went back to the kitchen for the tea. When I returned she was sitting with her head thrown back, eyes closed. She reached for a glass, took a long draft, and smiled contentedly. Then she said, "Oh! You had a telephone call." I had completely forgotten about Diana and the flight to London. I looked at my watch, it was 5 P.M. She said, "I guess it was your wife." She looked at me, amused. "Is it a secret? She didn't actually say. First she asked me who I was. When I said I was a friend of Ned's, she asked who Ned was. When I said 'McDonough,' she said 'Oh.' "

I thought that was odd, Diana knew who McDonough was. I waited but the girl said nothing. "Was that all?"

"She gave me a number for you to call in New York."

I nodded, looking at her. "What exactly did she say, when you announced you were a friend of Ned's?"

"She didn't say anything except 'Oh.' She said you could call Diana at that number, if you could spare the time."

If I could spare the time. I could hear her voice, the clipped mid-Atlantic accent that came with ten years in London. The accent would amplify her annoyance. "Maybe," I said. "Maybe you could characterize her tone of voice for me." We both looked at the telephone on the desk, the receiver crooked in its holder.

"I'd guess." She took a sip of tea. "Just the smallest bit hostile."

"Did you say I was in?"

"I said you were asleep."

"Good Christ," I said.

She touched the corner of her mouth with her finger. "It had the virtue of being true, what I said. I'd looked in on you, a man in a deep snooze, dreaming. . . ." She grinned and drank tea. "What could Diana have thought? Perhaps she thought you'd gotten loose in wicked Athens. Could she have thought that?"

"A distinct possibility," I said dryly.

"Does it happen often?"

"It never happens," I said.

"Well, then." She looked at me with her wide eyes and smile, and lifted her shoulders. "Well, then, it's a bagatelle."

"Should be," I said. "But isn't."

She looked at me closely. "It *never* happens."

"Hardly ever," I lied.

She picked up the telephone and handed it to me. "You better call her, bub. Sounds serious. The number is on the pad."

"I know the number," I said. Diana always stayed at the same hotel. I began to dial and she rose and picked up her glass and walked slowly out of the room, leaving me to deal with Diana alone. Guilty husband, possessive wife. I called to her, "You don't have to leave." She looked at me from the doorway, curious. I said lightly, "Sit down. Finish your tea." I had been married to Diana for eighteen years and any business between us could be conducted openly. I did not want this girl to think she had the power to interfere with my private life. I put my feet on the coffee table and waited for the connection to go through. But Diana was not at the hotel and would not return until late that night, New York time. That meant she was unreachable for another twelve hours. I left an affectionate message and hung up.

She lay full length on McDonough's soft couch, not moving, and I sat back and watched her, amused. Nothing about her reminded me of any of Ned McDonough's women. He'd spoken of French and Italian women, a Greek woman, and an assortment of Americans. But they were not this one, I knew that. This one was self-possessed and provocative, and I sensed a quick and subtle intelligence behind the assurance; she was not, I was sure, a part of Ned's *haute monde*. This one was undisguised, she wore no makeup and was dressed in a plain white shift. She looked at me now, suppressing a smile, knowing that I was assessing her. She'd asked, Do you work with Ned? And I'd replied, Sometimes. She seemed to understand right away that Ned's life and mine were not similar, and she'd asked no more questions. I thought I ought to tell her that Ned was the man at the table and I was the man in the backroom. What was there about my life that would appeal to her? I devised cease-fires that held. Truces that endured. I relaxed and sipped my tea, enchanted just looking at her stretched out on the couch, her hands one over the other on her stomach. I wondered who she was really, and what she was doing in Ned McDonough's flat.

I said, "Tell me about the pictures."

Her eyes popped open but she did not look at me. "How well do you know Ned?"

"Well enough," I said. "But I didn't know he had a family."

"They're in the United States." I said nothing, waiting for her to continue. "He doesn't talk about it a whole lot."

"He doesn't talk about it at all," I said.

"Then I won't."

I looked past her to a picture of Ned and his wife at a table in a nightclub somewhere. The photograph was grainy and off-focus, and I wondered when the picture was made. Ned and his wife were grinning gamely and toasting each other with champagne. I said, "Very mysterious."

"He hasn't seen them for years."

"His wife remarried?"

She shook her head, meaning No or I Don't Know; it was hard to tell which. She said, "How about yours?"

"She wasn't in," I said. "Won't be in until late tonight. You heard the conversation."

"Wasn't listening," she said. Then, smiling: "What do you suppose she's up to, in wicked New York?"

"Being wicked," I said.

"You don't believe she's up to anything?"

"Doubt it," I said.

"Well, you're probably right." She arched her back, staring at the ceiling. "What do you *do?* Actually *do,* when you're working with Ned?"

"I make cease-fires."

She began to laugh and her hand flew to catch my knee. She shook her head, spilling hair over her face. She was still laughing when she asked me if they were difficult to make. I replied solemnly that yes, they were extremely difficult to make. She sat up now, cross-legged on the couch, grinning. How long did it take to make one? I said it was a quotidian affair that depended . . .

"On a number of factors," she said.

"More or less," I said. "It's like making a suit of clothes."

"Ah," she said. And were the best ones made of natural fiber, silk or wool, or the synthetics? Rayon, polyester, Dacron. Did you ever make a doubleknit cease-fire? One that would never wrinkle or crush or tear —one that would hold its press for a generation?

Actually, I said, the skins of rare beasts were the best. Endangered species. Ocelot, alligator.

So they are expensive!

I said, "Invariably."

We were both laughing now. She was bouncing on the couch, her skirt hiked up in her lap, her eyes bright as gems and her small hands describing each new thought, as if she were conducting an orchestra. The questions kept coming between bursts of laughter. "I understand it perfectly," she said finally. "You and McDonough, I suppose your offices are on Savile Row. McDonough and Lyons, purveyors of cease-fires to H.M. the Queen. But what I want to know is, Who's the tailor and who's the salesman?"

I said, "I am the inside man."

"You make it and McDonough sells it."

"That's it."

She threw back her head and laughed. "McDonough takes the measurements and you cut the cloth."

"Exactly."

"And they last?"

"Most of the time. Sometimes. Sometimes not. It varies. Sometimes he screws up. Sometimes I do."

"How long has this one lasted?"

"The island? Eight days. Assuming that nothing has happened in the twelve hours I've been gone."

"How—" She put her hand to her mouth, giggling again. "Will you please tell me how you got into the business of making cease-fires? I assume there's no school for that, no Oxford or Cambridge or Sandhurst. I assume there's no institute located on Savile Row." She came off the couch and sat on the table in front of me; I could smell her hair, and the light scent she wore. "Please," she said. She was leaning toward me now, her green eyes staring into mine.

"What are you to McDonough?" I asked her.

"Friends," she said impatiently.

"You're not—"

"We're not lovers."

"Well," I began doubtfully.

"You're spoiling the mood," she said irritably. "You're just spoiling the hell out of it. Now stop it, and tell me."

I smiled. "I'm a lawyer."

"Right."

"I worked in New York."

"Yes."

"My law firm did some work for the organization."

"Bull!" she said loudly. "Those are things I don't need to know. I don't need to know them and don't care about them. I mean *why?* Tell me *why?*"

"I'm good at it. Some men make furniture. Some make money. Some are mechanics, doctors, soldiers. I'm good at this." I shook my head. "How the hell do I know?"

She smiled encouragingly. "Better."

"Look," I began, taking her tiny hand. She wore no rings, or any jewelry except for the one gold earring.

"We can get to that later."

"Well," I said thickly. "What do you want? Do you want me to make a cease-fire for you? I've never done it for individuals. I usually work with *nations*, you understand. Sovereign states. . . ." I wanted her to laugh again.

She asked, "Is Ned good?"

"Forget about Ned a moment."

"Is he as good as you?"

"He's good," I said. Then, "We do different things." She looked at me, her head cocked to one side, waiting. "Not as good as me," I said finally. She laughed and took two cigarettes from the box on the table, lit them, and handed one to me. "Look," I said again. She arched her neck, her face inches from mine. She murmured, "Um?" I put my hands on her shoulders, dizzy now with the smell of her. "Look, all this—"

"Much better," she said.

"Look," I said. "Do you want to go to bed or not?"

She smiled brightly and stood up, looking at me through cigarette smoke. Smoke hung between us and she waved her hand, dispersing it, still smiling, her head thrown back as if stargazing. "Ned told me that you were not seducible, but from the moment I saw you I knew that he was wrong."

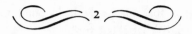

We did not make love right away that afternoon. The fiery sun disappeared and the air, cooling at last, became velvet. I opened the window in McDonough's bedroom and we lay together, talking. We were lying face to face and she said she wanted me to talk because she liked my voice, accentless and ragged. I did not know what was behind her, I was seeing only her surfaces. I began to talk aimlessly, fastening finally on a gangster I'd once had for a client. But somewhere in talking about that, perhaps it was the memory of the *mafioso* in my office, fingers clogged with diamond rings, I shifted direction and described my own career as an actor. I acted all through high school and college, *Boy Meets Girl, Misalliance, Winterset.* What I loved about acting was that, alone among the arts, you never witnessed what you created. A writer or painter sees what he does; an actor sees only the effect. Standing stage front I loved watching the audience, its attention or lack of it, its laughter or tears, and of course the applause. There was always applause, even for the most disorderly productions; at amateur theatricals no one is so churlish as to withhold applause. But it was not noise that exhilarated me, it was the expressions on the faces of those out front—watching, something I could never do. I suppose this was the first hint I had of what I would do with my life. That's to say, it was the *effect* that mattered; the result. The roles that interested me were the ones that made the play go. I loved the ensemble. I did not have the taste or talent for the Big Scene; it occurred to me much later that I didn't have the ego for it. It was a paradox, my amateur acting convinced me that whatever I did with my life, I would do it behind the scenes. I would be the one who made the thing go. An inside man, contemptuous of celebrity, measuring his life in result.

She said, "I don't believe a word of it."

I said, "It's true."

"You saw too many Gary Cooper movies when you were a kid. I know your kind—"

I had to laugh at that, maybe she had a point. Gehrig, not Ruth. "And you?" I asked. "What about you?"

"I went to McGill for a year, dropped out for a year, went back for a term, and then dropped out for good. I worked for an insurance company and last year my father died and left me a little money, and here I am. And here I intend to stay until the money runs out."

"You're a very beautiful girl," I said.

She ignored that, occupied now with tracing a line from my collarbone to my toes. She said, "No, not beautiful. But sometimes I am daring. And sometimes that is beautiful." Then she asked me if I was satisfied with what I did, making cease-fires. I said I was and asked her if she was satisfied, living in Athens.

She nodded. "Very satisfied."

"It suits you?"

"Um," she said. "But you. You might've been a great actor."

I said, "I can't see it."

"Well, not now. You don't have the face of an actor. It's a fine face, but it's not an actor's face. And you don't move like an actor, or talk like one." She put her hand on my chest. "And you're really happy now? Working behind the scenes with your organization, making cease-fires?"

I said, "Of course." Then, "Yes, seriously. I am." It was easy to become damp or sentimental about it, but it was true. I was a man lucky enough to have saved lives. I know that thousands of human beings are alive because of my efforts, pursued quietly and with no fanfare. In my line of work one success outweighs a dozen failures. The truth is, my career has encouraged idealism so long as I kept my expectations within limits. I am proud of who I am and what I have done, though I understand that it has taken a personal toll. Everything exacts some price. I asked her, "Where did you live in Canada?"

She slowly disentangled herself from me and lay spread-eagled on the bed, staring at the ceiling. "Saskatoon. Do you know how far from the back of beyond Saskatoon is? As far as you'd ever want to be, for sure. And cold. You do not know what cold is until you have waited for a school bus at six-thirty in the morning in the month of January. The trees creak in the cold. You're bundled in four layers of clothing. . . ." Then she began to move in rhythm to some tune she was hearing. She closed her eyes and began to whistle, almost soundlessly. Her hips pulsed slowly, her skin smooth as ivory and glowing in the fading light. I put my hand on her stomach, thinking her as singular and mysterious as the country she came from. I thought of her as teeming with life.

"Tell me more," she murmured. "Tell me about triumphs and disasters, stage center in a high school gymnasium. Tell me everything you can think of, and what went before." I listened to her voice, soft as fleece, and watched her mouth. And I began to talk, inventing stories, pausing every few moments to look at her, eyes half closed, mouth parted. Then the pauses were minutes long, and electric. Her arms went around my neck and held. I tried to look behind her eyes into her dreams. We lay together, tingling, kissing for minutes, holding hands like children. She opened to me and then we were making love in earnest and when it was over I was almost sorry.

I said to her, "Tell me about Ned."

"Ned is Ned," she said.

And I replied, "None of that." I gestured at the walls around us, the pictures of Ned and his family. The wife, the children; the house; the station wagon; the sailboat; the picnic; the portrait on the bureau. I asked her, "All that. What happened to it? Where did it go?"

She said, "They went home. They live in the United States now. She's an American born and bred. The children are being raised as Americans. She and Ned did not get along. Ned would never discuss that part. He moved out one day. He doesn't see them often and I've heard him talk about them only once. One night he got very drunk, and if you know him well you know that's uncharacteristic. He said she wanted to tame him and he wouldn't have it. It went against his nature. I think he hypnotized them out of his life, understanding that he could not live with the knowledge of his family split in two. You talked about him as the outside man, the one who sells the goods. Ned believes there is no Humpty Dumpty so shattered that he cannot put it together; *talk* it together if he can meet with it face to face. She'd meet with him all right but she wouldn't give. Anything. It's the way he's made, he walked out when some part of him understood that he would have to remake himself for the marriage to go. And he wouldn't do it. Ned puts one hundred percent into everything he does, whether it's working with you or making love to me."

"You said you weren't lovers."

"We're not," she said. "We never were. There's more than one way to make love and Ned's an expert in at least three of them."

"But abandoning your children—"

"He didn't, in his terms. Ned." She began to smile, hugging her knees. "Ned believes himself a hero. He believes that it's better that his children see him as a hero than as an unhappy husband, unable to come to terms with his wife." She smiled again. "A mere woman. Ned believes in setting examples. The exemplary leader, you know? And he understands that he has only one life and it's necessary to win with it. He believes in that just like you believe in cease-fires. And the pictures in this flat remind him of his promises. One trouble was, he married a woman just as tough as he was; maybe tougher."

I remembered suddenly a talk I'd had long ago with Diana. Marriages progress (I'd told her) exactly like a negotiation. First, general agreement on a few fundamental principles; next, the grappling with details. I thought then that the first two years of a marriage were critical, it was time spent defining the territory and the emotional range. Later on, there were fresh talks but the points under review were minor. There were adjustments of boundaries, restrictions on propaganda, agreements to move certain gun emplacements; but the fundamentals did not change. In that way marriages were similar to crises like Berlin or Cyprus or Palestine; negotiations only ratified an abnormality. Diana thought it a bleak analysis and did not apply it to us. I said, "What exactly did Ned say when you talked to him? And when did you talk to him? And why?"

"Last night," she said. "He calls me at odd times just to talk."

"And what"—I touched her forehead—"did he say about me?"

"He said you were dust wunnerful." I turned away laughing. She was a marvelous mimic. "He said you were using the flat for the night. I asked him who you were and he told me without getting into specifics. You two are very circumspect about your work. You'd think you were at Los Alamos, making atomic weapons. It's very irritating. He said you were up for some fun, but I was not to get any ideas."

"Because I am not seducible."

"The exact words."

"But you knew that wasn't true."

She said, "It was the heat."

"This morning," I said, "I was disoriented. I didn't expect to find a portrait gallery. And this afternoon I didn't expect to find you. Things were not normal. And you're right about the heat."

"That's the way, in Greece. Ned thought it would be a grand thing if I came over and made you breakfast. He said that I'd come as a bit of a shock to you but that you'd like it once you got used to it. And I did come early this morning, all prepared, but you weren't here."

"Plane was late," I said. Then: "I took the stewardess to Piraeus for breakfast, and then I took her to the hotel and came here. And the apartment was empty. Except for the damned photographs. Ghosts all over the place."

"How did you and the stewardess get on? Was she chummy?"

"She was Swiss."

"I'm glad, dear."

I laughed, her words carried a wife's tone and nuance. "She wouldn't say it that way, Diana."

"How would Diana say it?"

"I don't know. Not that way."

"Did you want to go to bed with the stewardess?"

"I would've," I said. "If it had been easy. I wasn't interested in making a campaign out of it." I looked directly at her. "I wasn't kidding this afternoon when I said it didn't happen. It doesn't. But Ned was dead wrong about the other." She looked at me without expression. "I haven't been through the preliminaries in so long—"

"Your wife must love that," she said dryly.

"—until today, with you, it's been a long time."

She said, "I think you're going to be very complicated."

"We'll be complicated together. We can carry each other's baggage."

She gave me a strange look, then smiled. "It's almost four in the morning. Call her now. I'm going to take a shower." She rose slowly and walked to the bathroom door and disappeared inside. I waited until I heard running water, but the room was still filled with her; her scent and spirit.

This time the connection was made. Diana sounded chilly over the telephone. Her brother had had a breathing seizure but he was all right now. She thought she would stay a few more days, returning to London on Wednesday or Thursday. Where are you? I replied that I was still in Athens but preparing to leave. I'd been up all night because the plane was late. But the housekeeper was on duty at home so there was no . . . immediate need. Who was the girl? she asked. A friend of Ned McDonough's, I said. Does this girl have a name? I realized that I had not caught her name. I had no idea what she was called. I laughed and said I didn't know; she was one of Ned's girl friends. Diana heard something false in my voice because she said she had to go then. A late supper with friends. I told her to cable me in London when she was arriving. She said she would, when she knew. Then I said, The hell with London. Meet me in Paris. We'd have a long weekend in Paris together. She was silent and I could hear the hum of transatlantic wires, and the splash of the shower in the next room. There was a very long silence. Then I said it didn't matter, we could meet in London on Thursday or Friday and go on to Paris the next day, or not at all. Up to her. Yes, she said, that sounded less complicated and more convenient from her point of view. I agreed, it was easier for me, too. I was mad as hell by then. She said she'd cable me her time of arrival when she knew it, and rang off. I sat a moment, thinking, and then I went to the bathroom door and opened it. She was washing her hair and whistling softly. I reached into the shower and turned off the water and looked at her a moment.

"I don't know your name."

"I said it but you didn't hear it," she said with a laugh. "It's Virginia."

"And I don't understand about Ned's wife. And the photographs."

She stood dripping, blinking at me. "Wylie, it isn't like the tide tables or a mathematical formula. It isn't easy to know. Life isn't always symmetrical. Marriages aren't. She left. And he saved all the pictures, maybe in the same way you keep a foreign-language dictionary even though you no longer use the language. Maybe *because* you no longer use the language." She looked at me shyly, her arms covering her breasts. "That's the best I can do."

I said, "Okay." Then I leaned into the shower and kissed her wet face and turned on the water. I had always thrived on complexity.

I have a friend who maintains that the virtues of marriage are visible only to people who have a profound sense of the future, and have seen successful marriages up close. His own parents had a very happy marriage. This friend believes in the marriage vows, particularly the one pertaining to adultery. He is forty-five, a stockbroker, and one of the nicest men I know. He says that restraint and fidelity pay "dividends" later on. Besides, the thought of an illicit love affair scares him to death. The thought of putting his wife, himself, and another woman through a "scene" appals him. But beyond that he has a vision of the future and the vision sustains him. He sees his children grown up and fortunate and he and his wife living quietly and productively in a temperate zone. He believes that when he is sixty he and his wife will look back on a betrayal-free life and rejoice. He is betting that the market will rise. I suppose in his own way he is betting on a counterrevolution. Charlie anticipates a day when, retired, he and his wife are sitting at the bar of the country club after a round of golf. They are sitting with other couples, friends, of their own age. Everyone has a drink too many and something is said and suddenly one of these couples begins to go at each other. Anger, tears; it is an awful moment, a resurrection of some ancient offense. I believe my friend lives as he does in order not to have a moment like that, when he is sixty. *Au contraire,* Charlie wants to look back on good times. He believes that a secure present depends on a virtuous past. Good times depend on good memories.

It is difficult to recount an upright Presbyterian life without sounding smug, unless you are writing about a saint or a hero, and my friend is neither. Charlie has a habit of laughing at mutual friends who live on the margins. *Him?* Charlie will say. *Him?*—speaking of a middle-aged friend lately seen with a girl, twenty. *Him?*— meaning that the standards of girls, twenty, have fallen since Charlie left the field. There's a note of regret in his voice but he does not waver. Whatever Charlie's personal life is really like, I cannot imagine that it is meaner or more brutish than the lives of these friends who live on the margins; or mine. All the evidence supports the worth of his view, though none of us can foresee the future and that is the heart of the matter. I once tried to joke with him about his theory, making sarcastic mention of dat ole debbil temptation—and to my surprise he agreed. He agreed it sounded mediocre and priggish and one could scarcely talk about it without gagging. But that it did not make it false. One must *resist,* he said heatedly, and for a moment I imagined him—incongruously, for we were lunching at his club on Wall Street—as an old Bolshevik on the barricades. I was forced to smile because the image came to me fully furnished, and I saw him in cloth cap and corduroy jacket and blazing red banner, this fastidious broker picking his way through the chef's salad and sipping white wine. He mistook my smile for condescension and immediately fell silent, embarrassed and irritated. I quickly explained to him about the image I'd had and when he heard me out he smiled and agreed that it was apt, though odd. He said that was exactly what he felt like, an old Red lamenting the death of the true faith.

"Christ," he said, laughing. "I'm an ideologue after all. Old Charlie, they'll never believe it in the locker room." We changed the subject then and talked of this and that, my business, his business, but after a few moments we were drawn back to our middle-aged marriages. We never talked in specifics, I am not comfortable in the confessional and neither is he. But at the end, as he was paying the check and we were preparing to leave, he said an extraordinary thing. "Of course, once you clear away the underbrush, women's liberation and hedonism and the rest of it, the heart of the problem is the death of romantic love. Marriage can't sustain it. Could once maybe, but not now. Maybe it never could. And we both know that we're romantic animals. If you don't get it one place you'll get it another. Try to suppress the impulse and you'll dry up like a prune. Indulge it and you'll end up in a motel somewhere with a teen-ager." He carefully signed the check and put it in the center of the table, the pencil placed just so across it, diagonally. "There's nothing in the contract that says it has to dry up, but it does —and I have a hunch that the reasons are identical to the ones that keep the marriage together. Civility, compromise, and a suppression of rage. People like you and me, we can't live in an atmosphere of perpetual turmoil. We're not made for it, so we find ways around it. I suspect that it makes us feel manly and capable to yield. I think that when we do that we hear the voices of our fathers, who were living in another epoch altogether. And of course we believe that nothing is perfect. That's a lesson we understand perhaps too well. We're reasonable men. My wife" —he smiled and pushed his chair back—"began to gain weight ten years ago. Not a lot, but it gathered around her hips and I didn't care for it. I told her so and she looked so hurt I never mentioned it again; I said, in fact, that probably I was wrong. Next day she began to tax me about smoking in bed, and we were at war for a week. But ah, Wylie. What minor complaints! What feathers on the scale! And I could give you a dozen more and you could match them, feather for feather. In some strange way it sustains me, seeing all these feathers as feathers. Keeping them firmly fixed and in perspective." He stood up and looked down at

me, smiling, his eyes bright. "Every week I send my wife a dozen roses."
We began to walk out of the club, it was now three o'clock and the place
was all but deserted. But he had one last thing to say, so we paused in
the center of that vast room surrounded by mahogany tables and pol-
ished silver and white-jacketed waiters standing at attention out of
earshot. "So we carry over one life into another. I broker my life as I
broker stocks. I've sold long, believing that the market will rise. You,"
he said, "have done the same thing. You've negotiated a cease-fire."

I was thinking of all that, waiting for Virginia to come out of the
shower. *Every week, I send my wife a dozen roses.* It was a wonderful
thing to be able to say, twenty years times fifty-two weeks of roses.
Charlie was playing Trotsky to Ned's Stalin, and what did that make
me? A modern man, an uneasy compromiser, I suppose I was—Khrush-
chev. Making my accommodations with the decaying West, sometimes
ludicrous; but shrewd. It depressed me thinking about it, so I thought
about Virginia instead. Virginia of the green eyes and smooth skin and
tiny hands, and brilliant laughter. Virginia from the outside; I did not
know yet what was inside. Just looking at her was enough to destroy the
habits of a lifetime. All weights and measures and the awareness of time
itself were redefined. Weigh it against twenty years of roses—and which
was the feather on *that* scale? At lunch in his club Charlie and I had
barely mentioned sex, that Geneva Conference of mediation and barter.
When he'd spoken of the death of romantic love he'd meant more than
sex; he'd meant elation and optimism and heat. Amazing sometimes the
way one . . . clung. I'd said to Diana once, Let us never negotiate out
of fear. But let us never fear to negotiate. I thought it was funny and
laughed. She thought it wasn't funny and didn't laugh. She'd said
evenly, "I am not a nation. I am a person. A human being with griev-
ances, and I do not believe that 'negotiation' is the word we should be
using." And she'd walked to her dresser and taken a book out of the top
drawer and handed it to me, and left the room to spend the night on
the couch. The book was a sex manual and in those days they were not
easy to find. They arrived by mail in a plain brown wrapper, and not from

the Book-of-the-Month Club, either. I read it with the attention that Metternich might give a high school test on the diplomatic art. However, in the end we did negotiate—what else was there to do? And my life followed the pattern of my work. Truce followed cease-fire and peace followed truce. But the two sides did not disarm. Far from it. The weapons were still there, whole arsenals of them. But they were not used. The threat of use preserved the peace.

"What did she say?" Virginia was in the bathroom doorway, drying her hair.

"That she won't be back until Thursday or Friday."

Virginia said, "Well, well." She perched on the edge of the bed, still ruffling her hair; little drops of water sprayed my shoulders. I said, "She was not friendly." Virginia nodded distantly, watching me. "And I don't think we have to discuss the matter further."

"Don't we?"

"No."

"I don't know," she said. "I'll let you know. I don't think I do, though. Why would I?" She looked at me with wide-open eyes and the tension dissolved. She smiled fleetingly and lay down on the bed. I was sitting up among the pillows and she was below me, legs casually crossed at the ankles, hands locked behind her head. I touched her shoulder, her skin hot and damp from the shower. She smiled again, deliberately, and turned away. Her cheeks began to redden and she closed her eyes. Her hand floated above my stomach. She was still smiling but trying now to disguise it. I gently moved her head into my lap and kissed her forehead, closing my eyes in order to imagine her; I wanted to see her in my mind only. She rubbed her knees together, then looked up at me. "I'm sexy," she said with a laugh. "I'm so damned sexy I can't stand it." She moved away and lay looking at me. We were lying apart, not touching; but what she said was true. You could see it, in her face and eyes and body. It was tantalizing looking at her. We kissed very gently and I could feel her lips and face tremble. I was trembling, too, with a great joy and release. Her spirit was flowering with desire, and inside me all the parched places were flooding. I did not know those places still existed and I gave myself over to them. I had not been conscious of them for a very long time, those empty places down the dark streets of my mind.

Later, when it was almost dawn, her eyes fluttered and closed. I had a terrible premonition that if I slept she would be gone when I awakened and I would never see her again. I touched her cheek and she moved closer to me and muttered something. She was almost asleep. I said, "Where do you want to go?"

She gave a little shake of her head. "Nowhere."

"I mean tomorrow."

She opened her eyes and looked at me, dazed. "What do you mean?"

I spoke very softly. "Let's go somewhere. You name it, anywhere. But not too far. Not out of this hemisphere. Not out of the free world."

"Anywhere?" She was waking now, slowly.

"Sure."

"Paris," she said.

I shrugged. "We can go to Paris anytime. Paris is a common place."

"Commonplace to you, big shot," she said. "Not to me."

"Okay," I said. "Paris."

"Have you spent a lot of time in Paris?" I nodded yes. "Not Paris, then," she said definitely. I waited as her eyes roamed the walls and ceilings and finally came back to rest on me. Her movements were languid, she was as fluid as a cat. I looked into her green eyes and she looked back. I thought I would help her out, so I began to name cities at random, Venice, Copenhagen, Nice, Amsterdam, Dublin, Rome. Then, joking, all the awful places, Birmingham, Bonn, Belfast, Mulhouse. She shook her head at all of them, she was thinking of something else. "There's one place," she said finally. "A museum I'd like you to see, if you haven't seen it. It's interesting, it would mean something to you. I know it would."

"Name it," I said. "We'll go there."

She said, "Barcelona."

It sounded all right to me. I had never been to Barcelona. "We'll go today if I can find a flight out of here."

"You're serious, aren't you?" I nodded. "This isn't some dumb joke that's been cooked up?" I shook my head. "We're going to go to Barcelona, I'll be darned." She sighed then, shuddering, and tucked her head into my shoulder. "I want to do it more than anything. I was there two years ago, alone, and loved it. One"—I could barely hear her now, her breath was light and hot against my skin—"dines very well in Barcelona. One"—her eyes were glazed and closing; I strained to listen —"loves very well in Barcelona." She pronounced it with the Castilian accent, Bar-thuh-lona. "And there's the museum, which I will show you. I will guide you through the museum, which I know intimately, and you will fall in love with it as I did." Then she was asleep and I gently put her head on the pillow and walked into the study. We had not left Ned McDonough's bedroom for twelve hours and it was strange to me, looking at our empty glasses and the two half-filled ashtrays. The flat was more ours now than Ned's.

I dialed Iberia and booked us two seats to Barcelona. Then I called the housekeeper in London and told her I would not be returning for a few days. I spoke to the children and they were well, unhappy at being awakened. I sat in the quiet room and watched the dawn rise over the balcony. When the phone rang I grabbed it right away. I didn't want it to wake Virginia. It was McDonough, "just checking."

"Well?" he asked.

"Well, what?"

"Did you meet her?"

"Yes. I met her."

"Is she there now?"

I paused a beat. "No." I could hear him chuckle. "We had dinner together and then she left."

"Right," he said. "Nice girl, no?" I said she certainly was. "I asked her if she'd go round to look in on you. Make sure everything was shipshape." I heard the chuckle again.

"Ned," I said, "you're all heart."

"Molz keeps me on my toes. Comrade Molz suggested I call Virginia, said it would do you good; nice Canadian girl." He waited for a moment, listening. "That's a joke, Wylie."

"Ha ha," I said. "What's happening there?"

"Some firing last night. Nothing important, except of course it means the cease-fire is technically broken. We're not acknowledging that."

"Casualties?"

"One KIA, a couple of wounded."

My heart sank. "God *damn* them," I said. "They knew this would happen. 'Made inconspicuous.' Horseshit! It was absolutely obvious, you cut the team in half, take Grandoni and me out of there, it was like giving them a hunting license. And we both know what will happen now. There'll be a probe tonight in retaliation for last night, and one tomorrow night in retaliation for tonight, and so on and on." I hesitated, disgusted. "Does New York know?"

"Of course," he said mildly.

"Hell, I'd come back right away if I thought it would help—"

"No," he said quickly, surprised. "They know the facts, they'll deal with it. Don't worry, Wylie. These things come unglued all the time, you know that. I think we can contain it. New York understands the situation."

"But New York is not *capable* of understanding—"

"No, that's true," McDonough said equably. "But they are the ones in charge, alas." He rang off then and I sat for a moment in the leather chair, watching the dawn and wondering if the island would explode after all. Perhaps it was cursed, exactly as the curator had said. I hated to think about it and briefly considered calling New York myself. But I knew that would be a wasted telephone call. I was not on the scene; Ned McDonough was. Suddenly I wanted very much to leave Greece, and was happy that in six hours we would be on our way. I smoked a cigarette and returned to the bedroom and stood watching Virginia. She was lying on her side, one hand where I would be, the other tucked under her chin, her hair spread in a golden fan over the pillow. I was not sleepy and simply stood there a minute, looking at her, wondering if she was dreaming.

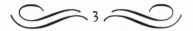

We arrived in Barcelona at dusk and went immediately to the Ritz. We bathed with a bottle of Champagne for company, then came downstairs to the lounge. There were only a few people in the lounge and from a ballroom somewhere drifted orchestra music, tea dancing. It was prewar music and the arrangements were Lester Lanin's. We talked about the situation in Spain. This was the period when Franco lay dying and Catalans were gathering in the streets, in suspense, hoping. We kept our voices low; it was discourteous to speak of the antichrist in the cathedral of the regime. We were excited sitting at ease, talking politics, anticipating uncrowded hours; we touched each other continually, no point was seriously made without a caress somewhere. An outsider listening to our conversation would have thought it lunatic, though of course we thought each other wonderfully witty and lucid. I think I have never been happier; our faces were inches apart and we were oblivious to the surroundings. I was telling her Franco anecdotes when the music grew suddenly louder. The doors at the far end of the lounge opened and starched men and women began to stroll toward us to the lobby. I stopped talking at once and we turned to watch this extraordinary *paseo*, reminiscent of matadors entering the bullring in full regalia. The men were mostly middle-aged and dressed in swallowtail coats and white ties; some of them wore florid decorations on their chests. The women wore black gowns with gloves, pearls at their throats. Cole Porter's music followed them, oompah-oompah, and presently a young man and woman appeared, the woman in a white wedding dress and train and carrying a bouquet. They stood a moment, both of them slim as sabers, looking over the lounge and those of us in it as if we were animals at auction. Then they commenced their promenade to the lobby. They walked very slowly, silent and erect, paying no attention now to us. There was an atmosphere to all of this, these well-bred Spanish faces in no way representative of our era; it was an antique show. The men wore their hair plastered to their skulls and the women were modest to an extreme, displaying no flesh below the neck and careful with their smiles. In the lobby they stood with the bearing of royalty, in conversation with the bride and groom. There was no obvious hilarity. Conversation for a moment was patient, then one by one they began to leave. A paso doble filled the lounge now as more people filed past, heads high and expressions proud. I looked at them and wondered if there had been speculation concerning the old man dying in Madrid and what it would mean for Spain's *treinta y cinco años de paz.* Franco's *paz.* She said, "All Spanish believe in miracles."

In a moment they were gone, leaving no trace, and we were alone in the lounge, listening to the dance band. I thought of those confident citizens of the old regime and imagined a bright cavernous ballroom, waiters gliding by with trays of drinks, the dance floor deserted but the orchestra continuing to play. We looked at each other and laughed and I paid the bill and we left, threading our way through those still standing in the foyer. Every man watched Virginia. She murmured apologies in a demure voice as we moved into the courtyard. We began to walk in the direction of the old city, and our restaurant. She'd made the reservations, it was a small place she'd visited the last time she was in Barcelona.

"I won a beauty contest in Saskatoon," she said, "and that got me to Montreal for a week. In Montreal I fell for an artist, believing that I could be his muse forever or for the season, whichever ended first. It turned out he already had a muse, Mrs. Artist, so it didn't work out entirely to my satisfaction, though I believe he remembers that week to this day. He ought to. My father owned grain elevators in Saskatoon and when I won the beauty contest he almost disowned me. A sinful thing, wicked. Beauty contest winners were 'whoors' in his opinion and as a matter of fact he wasn't far wrong. I was eighteen and after seeing Montreal I decided it would be a good thing to go to college. But the truth is, I'm not very studious or scholarly. There was no one thing that interested me more than any other thing, so college was a waste of time. And I hate to waste time. I do have an interest in Canadian Indians but they are better appreciated in the field than in a classroom. Facts don't stay with me but sights and sounds do; emotions do. My relations with men in Canada were not letter-perfect, the first man I was ever really serious about was a separatist from Quebec. My God, the meetings! We'd come home to the apartment after a movie and there'd be a dozen of them there, men and women, and they'd stay all night, arguing; it drove me nuts. They thought Quebec was the center of the universe and I knew it wasn't because I'd thought Saskatoon was the center of the universe and I found out soon enough that *it* wasn't and ditto with Montreal, the 'Paris of North America.' There is no single place in Canada that qualifies except certain Indian habitations and you have to be an Indian to know where they are. I have visited a few of them and intend to visit more, sometime in my life. Anyhow, they bored me to death with their ideological squabbles. They were then 'into' French anarchy, which I always understood to be a contradiction in terms. They were very cross with Camus because he'd had the bad luck to be born in Algeria. I suppose this gibberish comes from being a part of that great amorphous country, so loosely linked and so in thrall to outsiders. It's so big, Wylie, and so unimproved. Well, if you discover that Saskatoon isn't the center of the universe and then you find out that Quebec isn't either, and you have an ironic turn of mind, like I do, then you set out to discover what other places aren't. So I took my inheritance, which was not large but not small either, and went to Europe. That was a year ago and I believe that Europe isn't the center of the universe any more than Canada is, but it comes a little closer, and it's a lot more fun. And of the European cities I like Barcelona best. It's an ancient city-state, like Venice or Genoa." We were drinking coffee and looking at each other across candlelight. It was nearly midnight but the restaurant was crowded and noisy. "It was odd," she said. "My mother came from California but when she moved to Canada with my father it was as if her Americanness ceased to exist. Saskatoon devoured everything, it was the strongest culture I've ever been in. I mean by that the most definite, and the most exclusive. My mother never spoke of California except occasionally to mention her sister, who still lived there—lives there still —but whom she never saw. It was as if California were an unbridgeable distance from Saskatoon; it was the old world and Canada was the new. But she kept her United States citizenship, there was never any question about that. Though I have never felt the slightest bit American. Yankee." I lit her cigarette and she leaned forward, brushing my hand with her fingernails. "I have never had a relationship with a man that lasted more than a couple of months. I don't know why that is, unless it's a reaction to my parents who lived as if locked in an iron embrace. My parents never to my knowledge spent a night apart from each other; yet they were not especially affectionate and the house was not what you would call merry. It seems to me now that whole evenings would pass without the exchange of a single thought or emotion. There were no transactions in that house. Maybe I thought that was the fate of durable marriages: clenched teeth and short sentences. But my dear father died one June and my mother died the following October, a heart attack if you like symbolism. She followed him everywhere, even into the grave. To this day it is impossible for me to say whether they were happy together or not and I'm not certain that the question is even relevant. They simply were. Together. Is the shore happy with the sea? I know that life in Saskatoon was very hard, particularly their early years together; it was little more than a frontier. They were married ten years before I was born and I try to imagine what it was like, carrying a child in that country. A Californian living in Saskatoon, a spinster sister living in California; both parents dead." She paused then, her eyes turned inward; she was grappling with her memory. "I suppose I have been promiscuous in my relationships with men. I've never thought much about my body or 'saving' it. I've been careful not to be taken advantage of, and let me tell you I've got a loan shark's eye for when I am. If it's an equal attraction, it's fine with me, and if the man's a gentleman." I smiled at that, it seemed such an old-fashioned word. I had not heard a woman use the word "gentleman" in years and I asked Virginia what she meant by it. "It's in the dictionary," she said with a smile. "You can look it up. It's surprising how many men aren't. However, it's only fair to tell you that despite the artist and the separatist and one or two others I never had a completely satisfying sexual experience until I got to Europe and met a man of fifty-five who had spent his *life*, I think, in bed. Nice man, though odd. An easy man to be with, though he tended sometimes to order me about. I didn't mind it as long as we were equals in other ways. I seem to have an affinity for men older than I am. I think I'm attracted partly because of the baggage you carry around. At least, I am in the beginning. It's always difficult later on. I travel light and sooner or later you try to lay off your baggage on me, and I want to tell you now that it never works. Never. First place, I'm not eager to take it; second place, you never really let go of it. You just rent it out, like any chattel; you collect rent and retain the title. The odd thing about the fifty-five-year-old man was that he seemed to have less baggage even than me and of course in time he left, for a woman younger than I am. It was a liaison that was just about worn out anyway. It took me a week to get over it. I'm not made for broken hearts. That was a few months ago." I poured the wine while she lit a cigarette, silent now, looking at me over the candlelight. "Now you. I felt your presence yesterday morning when I was lying on the balcony. I knew you were there and I knew you were perplexed. Who is this girl? And I was apprehensive, too, though I was also being provocative. Ned had described you in very appealing terms. He said you were a man unaware of what was happening in your own mind but that he admired you, 'extravagantly,' he said, though you worried him. He said you had a weakness for the beau geste and naturally that tickled me because I do, too. But it's a happy quality in men. Anyway, I can't say why these things happen but when I saw you, blinking in that godawful heat, looking at me in a nice way, appreciating what you saw but not leering or making some stupid remark—" She laughed suddenly. "It was a thunderbolt, a *coup de foudre*. Then in the kitchen you were so nervous. All the utensils had to be lined up, it was as if you were arranging a regiment for inspection. If you said sorry once you said it six times. It irritated me at first, you had nothing to apologize for. Then I realized that it was just a reflex action and then I began to wonder about *that*, but by then . . ." We both began to laugh and I leaned across the table and kissed her, holding her a long minute. Then I summoned the waiter and paid the bill and we rose from the table, prepared to return to the hotel.

I said, "So you won a beauty contest in Saskatoon."

"First prize," she said. "Blue ribbon."

I said, "I have baggage."

"That's what Ned said."

"A portmanteau," I said. "And it's full."

"Well." She was smiling. She hooked her arm through mine and we began to edge between the crowded tables. "That's usually the way." I was leading and she came up against me, locking her arms around my waist. She said, "Maybe I'll buy part of it." I said, "It's all high-priced goods." She whispered the next words into my ear: "But I won't take anything on loan." In that spirit we hurried out of the restaurant and onto the street, bright at midnight.

I assume it is different now but at that time, some months before Franco's death, it was not easy to find the Picasso Museum. The regime had a long memory, which the artist did nothing to appease. It took us thirty minutes to find the building, a handsome brick structure on a side street near the docks. She had not told me what to expect but her enthusiasm was contagious and whatever it was I was eager to see it.

The museum is organized on historical principles, beginning on the ground floor with Picasso's juvenilia. There are very few paintings from his middle period and most of the very famous paintings are in other museums in Europe and America. I have always put Picasso in a special category of genius and it startles me to remember that he was born two years after Stalin and two years before Joyce and was an infant when Darwin died. I was accustomed to seeing him in the pages of *Time* or *Life* working in his studio in the South of France or surrounded by young women on a beach somewhere, his satyr's stance and grin captured in four colors; a man to admire without reservation, and his life did not lack joy.

We began on the ground floor, walking slowly, hand in hand. There were drawings in school notebooks and on the backs of envelopes, and I was enchanted to see that even as a child he had love for the female body and spirit. Women and animals, his charcoal line was always strong and supple. We paused in front of a portrait of a teen-age girl, this done when the artist was seventeen. It was the portrait of his sister. I wished suddenly that Virginia had sat for Picasso and I was looking at her, the open emotion of her eyes and mouth and the barely suppressed passion of her spirit; Virginia painted as she was now, in a plain white shift with the single gold earring and her hair careless. Virginia loose in white against a dark background. She touched my arm and we moved on, looking at the pictures on two levels, as art and as commentary on Picasso's life, because it was obvious that he was struggling with his own genius. There were periods when nothing seemed to happen, the artist content to occupy ground captured by others. Strolling through the silent rooms, I imagined Picasso's genius to be a ball of twine, Picasso chasing it like a cat, batting at it, trying to pin it down, ravel it, inspect it, and possess it. But it kept scooting away into awkward corners, he could possess it only a bit at a time. In one or two of the pictures I thought I saw something like despair. I turned to Virginia and she had a special smile on her face. I knew that whatever it was she wanted to show me, it would not be long in coming.

It happened then. We passed out of one room and into another and it was like witnessing a miracle. This was another order of experience altogether: *Woman with a Stray Lock of Hair, The Unbefriended, The Frugal Meal.* Picasso had found his theme and, standing in the doorway of that hushed blue room, dazzled and breathless, I thought only of a great army brought suddenly into battle, each unit behaving with discipline and courage, commanded by a supremely confident general. It was a stunning experience and when Virginia pressed my hand I could feel her own wonder and emotion. The pictures seemed to explode off the canvas, different from the ones we had seen on other rooms but connected to them, too. And this room was only the first skirmish, gloriously won but still a skirmish; Austerlitz and Jena were yet to come. We moved together trancelike from the blues to the roses and then, rounding another corner, to the center of our times. The artist had taken apart the world he created and put it together anew; physical forms, ideas, emotions, all history. The general had had himself psychoanalyzed by Freud and tutored by Marx and Einstein and was now a modern man, his art a definition of the epoch. I thought, foolishly, that it was like falling in love; the soul's door swung on its hinges. Nothing was concealed. We stood looking at the first Cubist drawings, then at *Las Meninas,* the maids of honor.

"What do you think? Doesn't it make you dizzy?"

"It makes me dizzy."

"What else?"

I said, "It makes me think of love. Loving. Being loved."

She said, "It's genius." We continued to stroll through the rooms and my excitement began slowly to drain away. The museum was filling now and there were visitors in every room, mostly Germans. I wanted to get away from it in order to think about it. I wished I had as clear a view of my own life as I seemed to have of Pablo Picasso's, or knew more precisely the quality of his resolve. Or the source of his inspiration; something beyond "genius." Where had he found his riotous music? I wanted to see my own life in periods of time, blue periods, rose periods; and understand the connections between them. I stood in the doorway looking back at the last maid of honor. Virginia said, "It's also ego-mania."

We stopped at the museum shop and I bought her a print of the portrait of Señora Canals. Then we were on the street again, wondering where to have lunch. Virginia said she had one last place to take me in Barcelona, but it was a sight best seen after a leisurely Spanish meal, four courses and plenty of wine. We could go where the meals were elaborate and the ambiance cheerful because if I thought the Picasso Museum a wonder, well, wait until we saw and scaled this other . . . phenomenon.

I was glad to be in the sunlight again. My emotions were still in a turmoil and I was only half listening to her. I looked around at this unfamiliar city and wondered for a moment what I was doing there. What was I doing in Barcelona? And who was this girl leading me through history? We stopped at a newsstand on the corner and I bought a *Herald Tribune.* And we were crossing the street when the map and the headline caught my eye. SCORES FEARED DEAD. I stopped in my tracks and she took my arm to hurry me as the light changed. I stood dumbly on the curb and read the dispatch, a very short wire-service bulletin. The details were sketchy, there was an "incident" and "firing" which had turned into a "pitched battle" near a tiny coastal village. I knew the village; the reporter had misspelled it. As I read the paragraphs my throat tightened and I felt physically ill. There was no mention of McDonough or Molz, only that the cease-fire had collapsed. Virginia was reading over my arm.

"Poor souls," I said.

"What does it mean?"

"That we begin again. From scratch. If they'll let us. Unless they find the killing too wonderful for words." Pedestrians were moving around us, annoyed that we stood on the curb. I put my hand on her waist and moved into a doorway.

"Why? Why would it begin again?"

"Because those *idiots.* In New York . . ." I didn't finish the sentence. I was sick at heart and there seemed nothing to say; this market would not rise. We stood for a moment, I was imagining McDonough and Molz trying to move between the lines, questioning their contacts, cajoling, pleading; they would have threatened except they had nothing to threaten with. I thought about all that and the many variations of it, and then I turned away toward the street. There was nothing I could do about the island. I was not there. I was here. I was in an unfamiliar city with an unfamiliar woman and I loved them both. The island was something else, inaccessible now; old baggage. I would not allow that to destroy this. They were separate parts of my life. I touched her cheek, she seemed more lovely to me than ever, standing in the shadows, her head tilted to one side, waiting. I kissed her once and then again and insisted we move along. I reminded her, there was one more sight to see. We could go to any restaurant she wanted, except that it had to be excellent and expensive. It had to serve Barcelona's greatest meal. Did she know of such a place? She nodded and I saw there were tears in her eyes.

"We're going to forget about all this," I said. She nodded again and tried to smile. I threw the newspaper into an ashcan. "Come on," I said, taking her by the hand. We began to walk rapidly up the street in the direction of the Ramblas. I wanted desperately to restore the earlier mood. This day was too crowded with emotion, and when I thought about it I was sad into my bones.

"Wylie?" Her voice was small. I stopped and put my arm around her waist. She felt weightless as she came up against me. I drew her gently to me and we stood a moment, saying nothing. Then I touched the tip of her nose and smiled. I was concentrating on her face, looking directly into her wet eyes and wondering if I could lose myself there. But my memory would not stop working, though I smiled and smiled. I realized then that I was squeezing her arm, hurting her. "That's better," she said sadly.

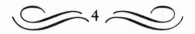

Lunch consumed three hours. We began with drinks and then we ordered wine, three bottles, and followed the wine with cognac and coffee. I thought that by drinking we could banish all the blues and to my surprise I found that we could. When the drinks arrived I began to tell her a little about the island and the work that Ned McDonough and I had done. I thought that the way out of it was through it. I told her how good Ned was and briefly described his technique. She asked me for examples and soon we were both laughing quietly. Halfway into the second bottle of wine I was nicely tight and knew that she was, too. The island slipped into the background. We were talking of ordinary things when suddenly she asked about Diana. What kind of marriage we had, what Diana was like, and what we did together when we were alone.

I thought a minute, then said we were suited to each other and not all married couples were. Obviously, I said, it was not 100 percent. But quite a lot depended on what you expected; her expectations and mine. She asked me to describe Diana and I replied that I wouldn't do that. *Ne kulturny,* I said with a laugh, though the truth was I wasn't sure I could do it. She said briskly that she understood that; it was all right. But she needed to know something. "The picture I have is incomplete." I told her that Diana and I were suited in practical matters and had been from the beginning. We agreed on the ways to raise our children and how to entertain and whom and how to live and where. We agreed generally about people. I have known too many couples who were unsuited in the practicalities not to know how important it was. Agreement in small things . . .

She glanced at me and laughed, not unkindly. "Important, is it?"

I said, "Very." She shook her head and mouthed no. "Is too," I said.

"Not small things," she said. "Big things. The primary passions. Maybe you can ignore them but I don't think I can. I know I can't. We can pretend they're isolated moments but we both know they're not. . . ." She went on in that way a moment, spirited and confident, sure of her ground. I was enchanted listening to her, though I felt myself pull away by inches. No reason now not to open the portmanteau and display my wares. I said I had a cynical story to tell her. She didn't have to believe it but she ought to listen to it. These were two London friends, their story. These friends had converted the primary passions into an art form. Not for them the Saturday night special, and while they made no particular boasts about their private life, they made no apologies or evasions either. They had an exemplary sex life. The trouble was, that was all they had. It was the only thing they agreed on. They disagreed about children, friends, vacations, houses, books, wine, and how much money was required to keep it all afloat. Dinner at the Burnses' was an agony of sarcasm and dispute and by the time dessert arrived Burns was sullen (and often drunk) at one end of the table and his wife was triumphant at the other, or vice versa. And leaving that house (seldom after 11 P.M.) one did not care somehow if later they manged to agree on the anterior or superior position to commit sex, each moving the earth for the other in multiple orgasm, it would be like admiring two goats. . . . I studied her slow smile and wondered suddenly what I was doing, defending the trenches of the Somme when my enemy possessed nuclear weapons. "Well," I said, beginning to laugh. "You have to know the Burnses to appreciate the nobility of the concept."

"What is that story supposed to tell me?"

"I don't know," I said. "Maybe that all Americans believe in miracles."

"I think that you are trying to tell me that the ordinary business of living. Is a firm that prospers. Isn't that it?"

I looked at her across the cluttered table. "It prospers until you fall in love."

She let that pass. "Describe the dividends. As long as we are pursuing this."

"They are not in excitement," I said. "Maybe they're in peace."

She said, "You can't believe that."

I looked at her closely, her face split by a thin ambiguous grin. How could she possibly understand the Burnses? They had been fighting for fifteen years, war was a natural condition; there had never been the slightest suggestion of disengagement. Diana and I had spent whole evenings wondering what kept them together, knowing that there had to be something besides sex. But there wasn't and we both knew it and the knowledge made us jealous and defensive. I was going to tell Virginia that it depended on what you were used to, or had become used to, and what you expected or were taught to expect or thought you ought to expect. But I didn't say that or anything like it. I said, "I used to believe it."

She was silent a moment, lost in thought. Then: "Do you know that there are only three intellectual pursuits in which people have performed major feats before adolescence? They are mathematics, chess, and music. Hard to say what connects them. A certain logic and order may. But there are no child poets, architects, or philosophers. I think it's because children are incapable of *desire*. It's different from just wanting something, you know. Desire and passion and ignoring limits in order to have them, or gratify them; *have* them, I think. They're so conservative, children; and of course they have no history to toss in the ashcan, when it's required." She leaned across the table. "Is it really war and peace? That's what you were saying a minute ago." I shook my head, that wasn't what I meant. She said, "I don't want to have a war with you. But I don't think I like the sound of peace, either. Not the way you describe it. Sounds more like confinement than peace, and I find it childish. This logical, orderly confinement—"

"The analogy isn't correct," I said.

But she wouldn't settle for that. "It's yours, not mine. If it isn't war and it isn't peace, what is it? You've got to *say* it." Her eyes flashed and she leaned back in her chair, intent now. She said, "You've got to say it yourself."

"The analogy's wrong," I insisted. "It's an easy analogy and it's wrong."

"Then there's only one thing it can be. The story of your life."

I nodded. "If you believe the analogy."

"Please say it," she said.

"Cease-fire."

"Do you love me now?"

I looked at her, all defenses gone. "Of course."

She touched my hand and we rose unsteadily and made our way to the door and the bright afternoon sun.

Where else do you go in Barcelona? The Expiatory Church of the Holy Family, La Sagrada Familia. We sat in a café across the street and drank a brandy, staring at the church, the sublime achievement of Antonio Gaudí, begun in 1882 and still not completed. It will never be completed, there is not money enough or time in all the world to finish this building. It is to stare into a mirage, bony spires spinning into the skies, an immense art nouveau facade, the stone incurved as if sculpted by a river's current. We walked through the side entrance, stumbling here and there because our eyes were on the spires. There were only a few visitors and, in a corner of the unfinished nave, two artisans sculpting a stone, working carefully with hand chisels, two old men working one immense stone, one of an unimaginable number still to be carved and fitted. We stood close together silently watching them and it occurred to me that I could watch these old men for the rest of my lifetime or theirs; this was an infinite undertaking, at the end of the twentieth century the nave would remain open to the sky. Gaudí's monument seemed to me at that moment to represent time itself, an eternal becoming.

The stones curved, and seemed to drip. Stone figures stared down at us from fantastic perches, and the spires soared dizzily overhead. I felt blood and alcohol rush to my face, and nudged Virginia. I said thickly that we had not really needed the brandy in the café and she replied that it was best to see La Sagrada Familia while intoxicated, the blood boiling. It was a conception so cuckoo and magnificent and outrageous;

it was not of this world, and therefore not best seen with a cold eye.

"I'm tight as hell," I said. She moved against me, her eyes on the cross atop the tallest spire. I dipped my hands in a helpless gesture. "All this . . ."

"Think about it," she said. "A primary passion. Nothing like it anywhere on earth. It derives from nothing, imitates nothing, suggests nothing, forecasts nothing. Nothing like it came before and nothing like it has come after. Absolutely its own kind, fully blown or fully flown. . . ." She began to laugh.

I said, "You're tighter than I am."

"Medium tight," she said. Then, impatiently: "Come with me." There was an ancient elevator that traveled halfway up the main spire. A winding staircase went the rest of the way up. We got into the elevator and Virginia said something to the operator that made him laugh. I looked at my feet and noticed my suit trousers were unpressed and soiled at the cuffs and my shoes were dusty. She looked immaculate. We alighted at the highest landing and stood looking over the nave and presbytery, the great porches and smaller spires to the rear, and the city beyond that. She nudged me playfully and indicated the operator, still standing in the open doorway of his machine. "Give him a peseta, lamb." I gave him five and he thanked me and took the elevator down.

We were alone in the damp silence. She stood looking at the city below us, breathing fresh air in great gulps. She rocked back and forth, testing the wrought-iron barrier. Then she turned flushed and grinning and began to climb the narrow spiral staircase, beckoning me to follow. "The view's better from up here, you can see forever, everything. . . ." She was out of sight almost immediately, I heard only her voice and her shoes scraping the stones. The stairway was enclosed, built into the stone walls, and black as a cavern. I said, "You go on." I was dizzy and very disorganized now, though I was standing fully two feet from the aperture. I looked out over the city, shielding my eyes from the glare of the afternoon sun. "Come on!" she cried, her voice faint now, disappearing as she climbed. I waited, afraid, standing back in the shadows. I did not want to follow her up the stairs. I realized then that I was trembling and forced myself closer to the railing. Looking down, I saw the city commence to spin and rearrange itself like one of Picasso's Cubist paintings. I shut my eyes and turned my face skyward, into the sun, praying for a breeze. I wanted to leave and looked around for the elevator but there was only the empty shaft. Birds wheeled and called above me. "Wylie!" Her voice came from a great distance and I could not locate it. "Here!" she cried. I craned my neck and looked up, leaning through the opening. She was fifty feet above me, waving from the highest window, her stomach pressed into the iron railing. She was balancing herself like a seesaw, smiling and waving. Her face swam in my eyes, high above me. I saw her fling out her arms and yell something and I turned away. I did not know up from down now and stood staring straight ahead, trying to get my bearings. Then I heard her familiar laugh, brilliant and sparkling above me. I looked up again but she was no longer there and my eye was drawn up the spire to a grinning Gaudí demon. Then she appeared, eyes alight, blond hair flying; she was balancing again on the railing. I knew then that she would fall and yelled to her to get back inside. Her laughter grew thunderously loud and she called, "Wyllllllie!" I leaned far out, motioning with my hands; the spire began slowly to spin. The world was going to pieces now. I pushed away from the railing and scrambled up the spiral stairs. Once inside I could not hear her; the heavy stones muffled all sound. The passage was narrow and treacherous, the risers wide on the outside where they touched the wall but narrow at the spine. My feet kept slipping on the stones, though I braced myself at every step. I was gaining, and after a moment I thought I could hear her voice. The sound of her voice was indelible in my mind. I imagined her face and body as I climbed, trying to see her now in my mind's eye. I thought she was calling and I rasped a reply. I climbed as fast as I was able but the steps were much steeper and more precarious than I expected.

I was falling before I knew it, tumbling heavily backward, landing on my spine. Then I was doubled over and falling. I felt a sharp pain and then nothing but surprise and wonder. My feet were above me at a crazy angle when my head hit stone and abruptly I was falling in slow motion, tumbling gently into the darkness, deep silence surrounding me as I floated in rhythm, the stones turning above me like graceful figures in a ballet.

Time held. Virginia drifted in and out of my vision, at last coming close to me. Her mouth touched my ear and she was talking. There were tears in her eyes and on her cheeks. She dried her eyes on my pillow, then spoke a few serious sentences, her hand resting lightly on my chest. When I woke she was gone. Later, Diana arrived, looking different than I remembered her. I believe she stayed a few days, then returned to London; she did not bring the children. I saw Ned McDonough the next day.

He could tell me nothing of Virginia's whereabouts. I remember him sitting in a plain wooden chair in a corner of the room, reading. I would waken and we would talk a bit. When the nurse came in he joked with her in Spanish. He told me I would be fine if I took it easy and did what the doctors said and tried not to remember too much. I asked him to find Virginia for me and he promised to look but she was an elusive woman and he could not hold out much hope. There were many cards and cables from friends. Ned read me a florid Italian greeting from the count and warrior Grandoni, and an undecipherable message from Molz. He said encouragingly, When you get out of here you can go to Athens and use my flat, if that is what you want to do. I shook my head no. I expected to go to London, after all that was where I lived. Diana and the children were there. He smiled doubtfully and made as if to go. I asked him finally if they had met, Diana and Virginia. He said that they had. And what was the atmosphere of the meeting? He paused before replying. "I would describe the atmosphere as 'correct.' " I wondered what that meant, in the circumstances. All of it was difficult for me to understand. He was at the door now, looking at his watch. I asked him what they talked about. I could not imagine what they had to say to each other. McDonough grinned and opened the door. "You, old boy," he said. "They talked about you."

"But why did she leave so suddenly, no word—"

"Wylie," he said, reproach in his voice.

"No explanation. No note, no nothing—"

"She knew you were on the mend. Of course she felt badly. I think she felt responsible."

I said, "That's cock."

He moved through the door, then paused. His smile was vintage McDonough, devilish and cynical and worldly. "It's the way they are," he said.

"Who?"

"The free spirits," he said. "All the Virginias. They only stay a little while but they always leave a trace." Then he reached into his pocket and tossed me a tiny box secured by a rubber band. Inside was the gold earring, the one that had flashed in the sun the first time I'd seen her on the balcony of his Athens apartment.

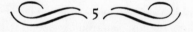

I was in the hospital four weeks, then released. On crutches I stood in the Barcelona airport, wondering where to go. There were flights to all the European capitals and the islands. I thought that a week in Ibiza would be agreeable but it was the height of the season then and I did not relish dining in the evenings surrounded by German tourists and their children. So I flew home to London.

The house was empty, as I expected it would be. I put my bags in the hallway and wandered through the rooms, a stranger. It had been almost three months since I'd been home. I wandered from the living room to the kitchen and finally into our bedroom, which doubled as a study. My desk was as I had left it; hers was bare. Familiar things were missing and her closets were empty. The children's room looked like any guest room, the beds carefully made and no clutter anywhere. The place was spiritless and looked to me as if no one lived there or had ever lived there. It was a house invented in someone's imagination, and then neglected. I looked through the dusty windows into the garden, badly overgrown but still recognizable.

I found the letter on the dining room table, addressed to *Wylie*, in her neat script. The letter said that she had returned to New York City, where she would stay until she found a place in the suburbs. She would take her brother out of the clinic where he had spent half his life; he would live now with her and the children, somewhere in Westchester. She did not know my plans but would like to, "for planning purposes." It would be easier for her and the children, especially the children, if she knew my plans. She hoped I was feeling better; I must have had a dreadful time of it. "I met your friend and I wish you luck. You'll need it." The letter was signed simply *Diana*. I stood in the center of the dining room holding the letter; then I let it fall. I walked slowly back to the bedroom. Everything of mine was where I had left it.

I made a cup of coffee and sat in the kitchen drinking it. After a period of time I returned to the bedroom. That night I tried a dozen ways to locate Virginia. There was no answer at Ned's flat and no listing for her elsewhere in Athens. I tried hotels at random, and Information in Paris and Rome and Belgrade and, for a reason that escapes me now, Helsinki. There was no listing anywhere. There was nothing at all, she had vanished. I have no idea what I would have said to her if I'd found her. Come back? Stay away? What happened that afternoon in Barcelona? What were we doing in Gaudí's towering spire? *What do I do now?* At length I gave it all up and lay down on the bed, aching. I ached in every part of my body. But sleep would not come and I lay awake until morning.

I went to work the next day but left at noon, exhausted. I did not return to the office for two days. When I went back there was nothing for me to do. A younger colleague had been assigned "temporarily" to the team on the island. I had my desk and my files and my secretary, but no assignments. My colleagues were extremely polite and deferential and I attended a number of meetings but there were no contributions for me to make. The circumstances of my accident were never discussed in my presence but were the subject of much office gossip, sotto voce.

Finally I was urged to take a leave. I had been back a month but it was obvious to everyone that I had not fully recovered, though I continued to arrive at my office each morning at nine. Then Ned flew in from Athens; they thought he was the one to convince me. He said that everyone was worried. You're the best in the business, he said, and we need you on the island but you've got to be fit. When I looked at him without expression he said he'd booked me into a small private hospital in Kent; "the best little hospital in England." He asked me if I'd talked to Diana and I said I had, three or four times since arriving back in London. She seemed happy in White Plains. The children got along well with her brother, the poor bastard, and vice versa. The brother was particularly happy to be out of the clinic. No, I said in response to his question, I did not plan to go to America. Ned's eyes shifted constantly and he seemed embarrassed. Then I remembered his flat in Athens, the photographs of the family I knew nothing about. I told him I was surprised that morning, coming upon his family. He looked at me steadily for a moment, as if appraising a combatant. "Know your enemy," he said quietly. Then, with vehemence: "You must know everything about them. Or I do. You don't. Isn't it strange, you don't need to know them at all." I allowed the silence to gather; the distance between us was immense. When I asked him about the island he looked away and shrugged. "About a hundred dead this week, both sides," he said. "That's fifty less than last week. I suppose." He smiled confidently. "That's progress, of course."

So I went to his private hospital in Kent. There was a French chef and wine with meals. I related my dreams and childhood memories to the resident swami. Each day I ransacked my memory and if nothing came (and frequently it didn't) I made something up. I remade my memory to suit myself and those imaginary connections were sometimes quite startling. Once I asked the good doctor if he thought I was telling the truth during our morning sessions. He looked at me carefully, expecting a trap, and said he always assumed his patients were telling him the truth. Why would they lie? I did not mention Virginia, assuming that he knew about her from other sources. This treatment was not supposed to be therapeutic. I was being analyzed in depth. You will go all the way down, the swami told me, until you can go no lower. But you can go lower and if you are brave enough you will touch bottom. When you touch bottom you will be well again, and in control. I felt no need to tell him that I had been there already, or what I discovered. He looked at me pleasantly and asked if I thought the treatment was helpful. I smiled and said of course it was. It was like a gift. "I am sending myself a dozen roses a week."

I signed out after three weeks; that is, I packed my bags and left. I was sick of the smell of roses. Everyone knows that my sort of disorder does not rise from an unhappy childhood or some long-buried trauma, nor is it revealed in nighttime dreams or nightmares. Still less is it corrected by a self-administered caress. It rises from the collision between one's public and private selves. It is an accident of history, this head-on crash, and naturally there is noise and confusion and injury, as in any accident. I have come to believe that we are stars fixed to certain courses, and those are not necessarily in harmony with the times; and that is the difference between good fortune and bad.

According to a postcard, Virginia has been traveling in Canada, visiting Indians she says; she has no fixed address, and hopes to return to Europe next year. She writes that her inheritance is dwindling; she gave away part of it to a tribe in Saskatchewan. "I have restored their faith in miracles." At night in London I think of Virginia and me alone in Athens and Barcelona, and of that remote island and the cease-fire I devised. Ned informs me that the island is quiet and there is now a de facto truce. The combatants are courting at last. The agreement we had seemed splendid at the time, a document at once humane and severe; perhaps it demanded too much. I search in earnest for the causes of the violation. I return to the island next week and it is essential that I understand what went wrong. I am composing a new pact in my head, taking all the fresh facts into account. I am writing a lyrical protocol, spacious enough to allow for human nature and strict enough to end the killing.